NA...

THE CASE: Track down the person stalking handsome TV star Rick Arlen.

CONTACT: Actress Mattie Jensen, *Rick's beautiful co-star on the soap opera "Danner's Dream"—and his ex-girlfriend.*

SUSPECTS: William Pappas, *the hot-tempered director who will do anything to keep Rick from leaving the show.*

Lillian Weiss, *assistant director and another of Rick's ex-girlfriends. She's jealous of his other romantic involvements.*

Dwayne Casper, *Rick's former agent, who still has a grudge against his ungrateful client.*

A crazed fan—*Rick's adoring public sometimes gets out of control.*

COMPLICATIONS: Nancy's friend Bess has fallen head over heels for the gorgeous TV actor—even though she's putting herself in terrible danger.

Books in THE NANCY DREW FILES® Series

Available from ARCHWAY paperbacks

THE NANCY DREW FILES™ CASE · 17

STAY TUNED FOR DANGER

Carolyn Keene

AN ARCHWAY PAPERBACK
Published by POCKET BOOKS · NEW YORK

AN ARCHWAY PAPERBACK *Original*

An Archway Paperback published by
POCKET BOOKS, a division of Simon & Schuster, Inc.
1230 Avenue of the Americas, New York, N.Y. 10020

ISBN: 0-671-64141-7

First Archway Paperback printing November 1987

10 9 8 7 6 5 4 3 2 1

NANCY DREW, AN ARCHWAY PAPERBACK and colophon
are registered trademarks of Simon & Schuster, Inc.

THE NANCY DREW FILES is a trademark
of Simon & Schuster, Inc.

Printed in the U.S.A.

IL7+

STAY TUNED
FOR DANGER

Chapter

One

NANCY, YOU'RE DRIVING me nuts! Would you please finish that sundae? Our plane leaves in an hour!" Bess Marvin looked longingly at her friend's dessert. Then she pulled a pink beret over her straw blond hair and reached for the matching pink jacket that was hanging on the back of her chair.

Nancy Drew looked at Bess, her blue eyes sparkling with amusement. "Take it easy, Bess. We're five minutes from the airport. George'll get us there in plenty of time."

Nancy and Bess were flying to New York City to visit Nancy's aunt, Eloise Drew, and

George was dropping them off. It was early, so they had decided to stop for ice cream near the airport.

"Admit it, Bess," George Fayne said with a laugh, throwing an arm around her cousin's shoulders. "You're just jealous because Nancy's eating that fantastic, splendiferous, mouth-watering—"

"Mmmm. And it's so-o-o good," Nancy said, licking her lips.

"Quit teasing, you guys," Bess muttered. "I swear I gain weight just looking at something that fattening."

"It does look good," George said, wistfully agreeing. She and Bess were cousins as well as best friends, but they couldn't have been more different. With her tall, athletic figure, her dark hair and eyes, and her levelheaded approach to life, George was her cousin's opposite in every way.

"When you two get back from New York, we've got to come here again," George said. "You can fill me in on your trip, and by then I'll be able to order something disgustingly rich and gooey. Just like those banana splits we had at that wonderful restaurant, Rumpelmayer's." George sighed. "I wish I were going with you."

"I'll never understand you," said Bess. "How can you pass up a chance to go to New York, the most glamorous city in the world, just so you can run in some stupid race? What's the big deal?"

"Don't be dumb, Bess. I've been training for this race for months. It may only be the River Heights marathon, but it's important to me."

"Yummm," Nancy savored one last mouthful of ice cream before putting down her spoon. "Okay, I'm ready," she said with a toss of her reddish gold hair.

Bess eyed the remains of Nancy's sundae hungrily. "No," she told herself, "I refuse to blow my diet before we even get to New York. I mean, you never know who I might meet," she said, looking at her friends. "In New York, anything's possible."

Nancy and George exchanged knowing smiles. Bess was sure to find cute guys in the Big Apple, just as she did in River Heights.

"Well, if I know Nancy," George said, "you two will probably wind up in the middle of an adventure. Remember the last time we were in New York? We didn't even have time to go shopping!"

George was right. Intrigue and mystery seemed to find Nancy wherever she went. At eighteen, she was already a rising star in the world of detectives.

"No way," Nancy protested. "This time I'm just going to be a tourist. I'm going to spend some time with my aunt, Eloise, do some shopping, see a Broadway show—"

"*A* Broadway show? Are you kidding? There are at least six that I'm dying to see!" Bess exclaimed.

"Hey, you two," Nancy declared, looking at her watch. "Now we had better hurry."

And with that, the three girls paid their bill and filed out of the ice cream shop.

"Here we are," Bess said, staring up at the elegant old apartment building. "This street always looks like a movie set of 'old New York' to me. Like it's a hundred years old, at least."

It was true, Nancy thought. The street had old-world charm, from the tall gingko trees with their fanlike leaves to the old-fashioned gas lamps along the sidewalk that fronted the many brownstone buildings.

"Did I tell you my aunt bought her apartment last year when— Oh, look, there she is!" Nancy cried, waving to her aunt, who was coming out the front door. Tall and elegant, Eloise Drew was a female version of Nancy's father, Carson. They had the same lustrous brown hair and aristocratic features.

"Nancy!" Eloise cried, hugging her niece warmly and planting a kiss on her cheek. "I'm so happy to see you! And Bess," she said, taking Nancy's friend warmly by the hand. "How good it is to see you again. How was your trip?" Eloise asked as they entered the building.

"Kind of boring," Bess admitted with a smile.

"Wonderfully uneventful is more like it," Nancy said in the elevator up to Eloise's second-floor apartment. "I've been so busy lately that it was great just to sit down and leaf through a magazine."

"Well, here we are!" Eloise said, pushing open the door to her apartment. "I've redecorated a bit since you were here the last time."

The apartment was spacious and homey. Bright sunlight splashed across the walls, which were papered in a dainty flowery print.

"I love what you've done!" Bess exclaimed enthusiastically as they were passing through the living room. She paused to look out the window. "I had forgotten there were trees in the backyard!"

"In New York we call it a courtyard. Unfortunately, though, as you probably remember, your room faces the street." Nancy's aunt led them across a small hallway to a cozy bedroom. "Don't worry, the street is usually pretty quiet."

Just then a fire engine came careening down the block, its siren blasting. Eloise waited for it to pass before adding, "Quiet for the city, that is."

The room was all ready for the two girls. Both beds were freshly made with light blue comforters, and two sets of fluffy white towels were neatly folded on top of the modern oak bureau. Eloise slid open a pair of white louvered doors, revealing a nearly empty closet.

"Here you are, ladies," she announced. "And after you've unpacked, we'll have a snack. For dinner, I thought we could go to my favorite Chinese restaurant."

"Super," Nancy said, looking over at Bess, who seemed enthusiastic. "As long as there's no mystery involved, I'm game for anything."

"Well—" Nancy's aunt said hesitantly. "I wouldn't go so far as to say 'no mystery,' Nancy. I was going to save it for later, but since you brought it up . . ."

"Oh, no! I don't want to hear another word. I'm here for a week's vacation, and that's that!" Nancy flung herself on the bed and covered her head with a pillow.

"Okay, okay." Eloise shrugged. "I only thought you'd be interested because it has to do with a TV show. . . ." She stared absently at the ceiling, showing no emotion.

"What TV show?" Bess asked. Nancy's aunt didn't answer. "Come on, Nancy, ask her. I've got to know!"

Nancy peeked out from under her pillow, looking back and forth from Bess to Eloise. "Okay, Aunt Eloise," she muttered. "I give in. What show?"

"Well, let me start at the beginning," the older woman replied, sitting down next to

Nancy. "Yesterday, I happened to tell my downstairs neighbor you were coming to stay with me. Her name is Mattie Jensen, and she's an—"

"The Mattie Jensen? Of 'Danner's Dream'?"

Eloise nodded, and Bess nearly fainted with excitement.

"I don't believe it! Mattie Jensen is your neighbor! Is she as beautiful in real life as she is on TV? Is she anything like Serena Livingstone?"

"Hey, wait." Nancy propped herself up on one elbow, looking bewildered. "You guys are way ahead of me! Who's Serena Livingstone?"

Bess looked at Nancy as if she had just arrived from Mars. "That's Mattie Jensen's character on 'Danner's Dream.' Gosh, Nancy, you're really out of it. You at least know who Rory Danner is, don't you?"

Nancy shook her head.

"His real name is Rick Arlen. He and Mattie are the stars of the show," Eloise explained. "Anyway, I told her that you're a detective, and she got very excited."

"Well, is she?" Bess persisted. Nancy and Eloise looked at her, puzzled. "As beautiful in real life, I mean. And as together as Serena?"

"Oh!" Eloise laughed. "Well, let's see. If anything, I'd say she's more beautiful in person. As for together—well, Mattie's a sweet

7

girl, but she's very emotional. I guess you could say she has an artistic temperament."

Eloise turned back to her niece. "Anyway, she was really hoping you would stop by the set. It seems some strange things have been happening to Rick Arlen. She said she could get both of you guest passes for tomorrow morning. If you're willing, that is."

"*If* we're willing? Of course we are!" Bess declared. "I can't believe I'm going to visit the set of 'Danner's Dream'! Wait till George hears about this! She's as crazy about Rick Arlen as I am."

"Don't tell me George watches 'Danner's Dream,' too," Nancy cried in surprise. George was always either training for some athletic event or lost in the pages of a book. How could she have time to watch daytime TV?

"Her mother tapes it for her," Bess explained. "Everybody watches Serena and Rory. They're the hottest couple on the soaps!"

"I think I have heard of them, actually. He was featured in *Chatter* magazine last month, right?" Nancy asked.

Bess nodded. "Blond hair, dazzling blue eyes, muscles out to here," she said, indicating large biceps. "Need I say more?"

"I get the picture," Nancy replied. "But I promised myself—*no mysteries.*"

"Oh, come on, Nancy. How many chances do you get to meet real stars?"

"Well, it would be kind of interesting to see how a television show is put together—"

"Interesting?" Bess cried. "It'll be fantastic! I'll die if we don't go!"

"Then I guess I *can't* say no, can I?" She turned to her aunt. "Okay, you can tell your neighbor we're on."

"Great," said Eloise. "Mattie said you could show up at the studio around ten."

"All right!" Bess exclaimed, her light blue eyes dancing. "Now, I've just got to decide what to wear tomorrow."

"I'd rather check out that snack you were talking about, Aunt Eloise."

"Wait a minute!" cried Bess. "I'm coming, I'm coming. I'll pick out my clothes later."

Nancy had to laugh. Bess was so excited. She just hoped that Mattie Jensen was as prone to exaggeration as Aunt Eloise had said she was. If so, how much of a mystery could there really be?

"Are you sure this skirt fits?" Bess asked. She and Nancy had just walked through the huge glass doors of Worldwide Broadcasting.

"You look fabulous," Nancy assured her friend. All morning Bess had been fussing in front of the mirror, getting ready for their visit to the set of "Danner's Dream." And the results were definitely worth the work. In her soft suede skirt, tights, and ankle boots, Bess looked like a star herself.

"Okay, people," a voice behind them shouted. "We go in here! Make sure your guest pass is visible."

Nancy turned and saw a group of about thirty people push through the same glass doors she and Bess had just entered.

"It's okay, Harry," the tour guide in a navy blue uniform called to the security guard. "They're with me."

"Where you going? 'Danner's Dream'?" the guard asked.

"You guessed it," replied the tour guide.

"It's going to be a zoo in there today," the guard muttered. "But whatever— Management must know what they're doing. Take them into studio one, Joe."

"Well, if I were Serena, I'd kill him," Nancy heard a woman in the tour group say. "I mean, who does that Rory Danner think he is?"

"They may *have* to kill him," her companion replied. "I heard he's leaving the show at the end of the season."

"No!"

"Yes! Didn't you read the *Star Sentinel* last week? He wants to break his contract to make a movie."

"Well, if you ask me, Rick Arlen has gotten

too big for his britches," the first woman said. "We fans count, you know."

At the rear of the group was a large man in an old sweatshirt. He was shifting from foot to foot and muttering, "You'll find out, Rory. You're not that great."

At last they all disappeared through a set of swinging doors. "Boy, they sure seem angry," Nancy remarked.

"That's nothing," the security guard said. "Ever since Arlen decided he was leaving the show, seems like everybody hates him. I wouldn't want to be him right now, no siree." He shook his head. "Can I help you girls?" he finally asked.

"We're here to see Mattie Jensen," Nancy said politely. "She's expecting us."

The guard checked his book. "Miss Drew and Miss Marvin?" he asked. "Let's see—ten o'clock . . . she's probably just going into makeup. It's down the hall and around to your right. First left after the producer's office."

Thanking him, the girls made their way through the set of swinging doors that led into a long hallway. The noisy tour group had gone directly onto the set, but Nancy and Bess continued on, looking for the makeup room.

"This must be the hall he means," said Nancy.

"Maybe we'll pass the casting director's office," Bess whispered, following her.

Just then, two young secretaries stepped into the hall ahead of them. "Well, I think he has a good point!" one was saying to the other.

"He may have a point, but that's still no way to talk to people. Even if he is the producer!"

Feelings seem to be running high everywhere, Nancy thought. Suddenly she grabbed Bess by the wrist and signaled for her to be quiet.

They stopped by an open door with a sign that read William Pappas, Producer. They couldn't see in or be seen. Inside, a man was shouting, probably into a phone since no one responded to him. "I've told you before, he can't do this to me! I don't care if he *is* Rick Arlen. If he leaves this show, he'll never work again! Nobody—*nobody*—breaks a contract with me. I'll kill him before I let him work for someone else!"

Chapter
Two

"I CAN'T BELIEVE he feels that strongly about Rick Arlen," Bess whispered angrily.

Nancy peered into the office, taking care to remain hidden. William Pappas's face was flushed with anger as he stared at the phone he had just slammed down. He fumbled in his pocket for a cigar.

"Actors! They're all alike! No class—none at all," he muttered to himself. Then he rose and shouted to a timid-looking girl in an inner adjacent office. "Get the writers on the phone and tell them I want a Rory Danner death scene—the more realistic the better. That idiot doesn't deserve to live after what he's put me through! And where's my Danish? You know I can't think before I've had my second coffee."

"Come on!" Nancy said in Bess's ear. "Let's get out of here." They hurried down the long hallway without looking back.

"Gosh, Nancy," Bess announced after they'd rounded a corner and were safely out of sight, "I'll bet he's the one who's causing all the trouble."

"I don't know, Bess. Maybe he has an artistic temperament, too. Remember what my aunt said about Mattie Jensen?"

Bess's attention, however, was caught by something else. "'Makeup.' Here we are." Bess placed her hand over her heart. "I can't believe I'm about to walk through that door and meet Mattie Jensen! How do I look? Are you sure this skirt is okay?"

Nancy couldn't help laughing. "You're too much," she said teasingly. "It *still* looks great, but if you're so uncomfortable why did you wear it?"

"Because it looks great—you just said so yourself!" Taking a deep breath, Bess knocked on the door.

"Come in," someone called out. Bess immediately recognized the voice of her favorite soap opera character.

Inside, Mattie Jensen was sitting in a large, barber-style chair. Her famous auburn curls were wrapped in purple curlers, and her porcelain skin was scrubbed clean. Not a hint of makeup anywhere. But she still looked incredibly beautiful, and her green eyes sparkled.

"Mattie J-Jensen," Bess sputtered.

"You must be Nancy Drew," Mattie replied. She held out a manicured hand and gave Bess a warm smile.

"No, I'm Bess Marvin. She's Nancy."

"Oh, of course," Mattie corrected herself, taking Nancy's hand. "It's great to meet both of you."

"Thanks, same here," Nancy answered.

"Nancy, Bess, I'd like you to meet Kay Wills. She's our makeup artist and one of the great ones. Without her, I'd be lost."

"Come on, Mattie, don't be so modest." Kay rolled her eyes at the girls and began dotting ivory base on Mattie's forehead. "With looks like yours, you'll never be lost."

"Well, looks aren't everything, are they?" Mattie sighed, holding her head still as Kay blended in the foundation.

"Try telling that to your leading man," Kay sniffed, continuing to work.

"Poor Rick," Mattie murmured. "He's so misunderstood. And now all this awful stuff is happening to him. Nancy, maybe you'll be able to help."

Nancy leaned against the wall. "To be honest, Ms. Jensen, I'm in New York on vacation.

I really don't want to get involved in anything complicated."

"Please, call me Mattie. And you've got to help him, Nancy! It's a matter of life and death!"

"You know, you're a lot more upset than he is, Mattie," Kay put in. "As far as I can tell, he loves the attention, no matter how negative it is."

Nancy was puzzled. "If you tell me what's going on, maybe I could give you a few suggestions," she offered. After all, she told herself, giving advice was different from actually getting involved.

"Didn't Eloise tell you?" Mattie asked frantically, her luminous eyes filling with tears. "Someone is trying to kill Rick!"

"Don't cry," Kay ordered, dabbing Mattie's eyes with a tissue. "You'll ruin your makeup."

"Sorry. It's just so upsetting."

"Maybe you should start at the beginning," Nancy said, taking an empty chair next to Mattie.

"It began with the chocolate," Mattie explained, leaning forward. Kay chased after her face with a powder puff. "A box of it came in with the rest of the fan mail one day. Rick is a maniac for chocolate, so he opened the box and ate one right away. It was so bitter that for a minute he thought he'd been poisoned. After a while, though, when he didn't keel over, he figured it was just a practical joke. We all did. But then a letter arrived. It said something like, 'Scared you, didn't I? Good, because this was just a dress rehearsal.' About two days later, a watch came in the mail. It was set at five to midnight, and there was a note attached that said, 'Your time's running out.' You see? Somebody is trying to kill him!"

Mattie was practically standing up in her chair. Kay gently pushed her back down and began working on her eyes. "Take it easy, hon," she said matter-of-factly.

"Maybe this is a stupid question," Nancy ventured, "but has anybody called the police?"

Kay laughed. "If we called the police every time we got a nasty letter around here, we'd be calling them every day! You should see some of the fan mail."

Mattie wheeled around in her chair. "But this is different! These aren't just nasty letters, they're real threats! The trouble is, nobody is taking them seriously!"

"Not even Rick?" Nancy asked.

"Especially not Rick," Mattie said huffily. "He thinks nothing will ever hurt him. As far as he's concerned, the whole thing is the work of a single loony fan out for kicks. I'm the only one who's really worried, and that's why I need your help."

"She'll help you, won't you, Nancy?" Bess

said, not really asking the question. "We'll stay here as long as it takes!"

Nancy smiled wryly. Bess would have promised anything if it meant she could spend more time with her idols.

"But, Bess," she said, protesting. "We have a lot of sightseeing planned, and—"

Just then, the door flew open and Rick Arlen burst in. Bess gasped. He really was even more gorgeous in person. A lock of blond hair had fallen over his forehead, and he impatiently brushed it away. He was holding up a black-and-white glossy photograph of himself. The photo had been scratched almost beyond recognition.

"Mattie," he said, thrusting the picture into her hands, "it's happened again! Look at this!"

Mattie looked at the photo, and at the message scrawled beneath it. " 'If you won't be mine, you won't be anybody's,' " she read. She looked up at Nancy. "You see what I mean?"

"At least it's an old picture," Rick said, trying to make a joke. "It's not even very good, actually."

Bess was standing, absolutely frozen, staring moronically at Rick. Noticing her obvious interest, Mattie hastily introduced the girls to Rick, but it was clear that his mind was on other things. He hardly noticed them.

"Whoever did this has some nerve," he was

saying. "Imagine, tearing up my face like that."

"Please, Rick," Mattie begged, "if you won't call the police, will you at least tell security about this?"

"Come on, now," he said, waving away her concern. "What are they going to do about it? Shake their heads and wring their hands, that's what. Anyhow, it's probably just old man Pappas trying to scare me."

"Rick!" Mattie gasped. "You don't really think—"

"I don't know what to think," he muttered with a shrug. "All I know is that we're scheduled to be on the set in five minutes for dress rehearsal, and I haven't got time for nonsense like this." Rick turned toward the door. Jaw set, eyes ablaze, he was the picture of that perfect romantic rebel, Rory Danner. "See you on the set, Mattie. Oh, and nice meeting you, girls."

He gave Bess and Nancy a cursory nod as he left the room. "What a hunk!" Bess whispered hoarsely. "Oh, Nancy, you've just got to take this case! Just think what might happen to Rick if you don't."

"Bess, sick as it might be, sending hate mail is not a felony."

"Please," Mattie said, breaking in. "Something's very wrong here, I'm sure of it. I'd feel so much better if you'd at least stay and watch this morning's dress rehearsal."

Nancy looked from Mattie to Bess and back again. There was no way they would let her say no. Besides, she reasoned, watching a soap rehearsal was kind of like sightseeing, wasn't it? "Okay, we'll stay," she agreed.

"Oh, Nancy!" Mattie cried happily. "You won't regret this! I promise!"

Nancy hoped not. But she couldn't get rid of the depressing feeling that for the hundredth time, a relaxing vacation was about to be ruined.

On their way to the set, Nancy filled Mattie in on what she and Bess had overheard outside Pappas's office.

"Those two are really on the outs these days," Mattie said. "Ever since Rick got that film deal and gave his notice, it's as though a war has been declared between them. I can't really blame Mr. Pappas, though. The show's ratings depend on Rick. If he goes, 'Danner's Dream' could be in big trouble, and that means trouble for all of us."

"Hmmm." Nancy thought for a moment. "So it's not just Mr. Pappas who's down on Rick."

"Oh, no. In fact, lately it's been Rick against the world." She stopped. "Well, here we are."

Mattie pushed against a vacuum-sealed door. With a *whoosh,* it opened, and the three of them walked onto the set.

Nancy and Bess gazed around the massive studio. In straight rows, rooms that had three walls but no ceilings were set up. Rows of klieg lights hung on suspended bars. Above the lights was a narrow catwalk, and above that, total darkness.

On the ground level, the activity was incredible. Hundreds of cables wound across the floor, and several huge cameras were mounted on dollies. Each one was surrounded by people. On the set of the Danner living room, where the first scene was about to be shot, set dressers were putting the final touches on the scenery. And in the middle of it all stood Rick Arlen. Kay was fussing over his makeup, and he was going over his lines with a script girl. But in case he or anyone forgot a line, a teleprompter stood in either corner of the room. All an actor had to do was cast a glance at one of them and read his lines from the screen.

Nancy and Bess were struck by the strangeness and complexity of it all. They looked dazed as Mattie motioned them to a spot on the floor where they could watch the rehearsal and still be out of the way. Then she disappeared behind the walls of a set.

21

"Can you believe this?" Bess whispered excitedly.

"Could somebody tell Rick to get on the set, please?" A beautiful black-haired woman barked impatiently into a small megaphone.

"I'm right here, Lillian, dear," Rick purred sarcastically. "What would you like?"

"I hope you bothered to memorize your lines," she snapped.

"Yes, love, I did," he cooed.

"That's what you always say," she said, trying too hard to keep the anger out of her voice. "You shouldn't need a teleprompter, Rick. You're a big boy and a professional."

"If you're referring to that one small incident, Lillian, you'll also recall that I received a death threat that morning. It wasn't exactly my best day."

Suddenly a voice boomed over the set's sound system. "Lillian, back off, will you?"

"Who's that?" Nancy wondered out loud.

A bearded stagehand who was walking by with a line of cables answered her. "That's Luther Parks, the director. He's up there." The stagehand pointed to a Plexiglas booth above the door at the back of the room. "He watches the rehearsal on a bank of TVs up there, and then chooses which camera shots they'll use."

"And who's Lillian?" Nancy asked.

"Ready to roll, ladies and gentlemen," the

director's voice interrupted them. "Let's have quiet on the set, please."

"Places, everyone!" the stage manager yelled. "Charlie, are we locked up?" The man at the door nodded. A bright red light went on above him.

"That light means we're shooting," the same stagehand explained in a soft whisper. With a quick smile, he was gone.

In the silence of the huge studio, Nancy could feel the crackling of tension. For a split second no one moved. Then Rick appeared on the set and sat down on the beige sofa in the Danner living room. With his head in his hands and his elbows on his knees, he looked just like the tortured Rory Danner, brooding over his life. Then Mattie, playing the cool and dignified Serena, appeared in the living room doorway.

"Rory?" she called out softly. "May I come in?"

Rick looked up, but then dropped his head back into his hands. "I don't want to see you, Serena," he growled. "Just get out and leave me alone!"

Mattie stood by the door, cold as ice. "Rory, I have to talk to you—right now." The cameras rolled in for a closeup.

Just then, Nancy noticed a faint shadow moving back and forth on the back wall of the

23

set. She glanced up to see what was causing it. High overhead, she saw a klieg light wobbling wildly on its track. Horrified, Nancy watched as it broke off the bar with a sickening snap and hurtled downward. It was heading right for Rick!

Chapter

Three

NANCY STOOD UP and dove across the set, landing on top of Rick. The sofa beneath them toppled over backward. Everyone watched in frozen terror as the heavy lamp hit the floor where the couch had been, shattering into a thousand pieccs.

Moments later pandemonium broke out as the cast and crew gathered around the scene of the disaster. Mattie rushed up to Nancy and Rick, who were still in a heap on the floor, gasping for breath.

"Rick! You could've been killed!" Mattie cried. The stage manager was calling for everyone to remain calm on the set, and Bess tried to push her way through a group of stagehands. She stretched, looking to see if Nancy and Rick were okay.

"What in the world is going on around here?" William Pappas hurried onto the set, pushing people aside as he went. "This is all I need! Our insurance rates are high enough as it is!" he muttered angrily. "Is anybody hurt?"

"Nope," Rick replied from his position on the floor. "I was just rescued by this beautiful creature." He looked up at Nancy with a grateful smile. "Hello, gorgeous. Where have you been all my life?"

Nancy turned red to the roots of her hair as she scrambled off Rick and onto her feet. Brushing herself off, she started to push her way through the crowd of onlookers. She had to find Bess.

"Wait!" Rick called after her. "Don't leave me now!" With that, a group of stagehands who were standing nearby broke out in nervous laughter.

Just then Nancy felt a hand on her shoulder. It was Mattie. "Thank heavens you were here. If you hadn't gotten to Rick so quickly . . ." She shivered. Turning to the crowd, she called out, "Everyone, I'd like you to meet Nancy Drew. She's my guest today." Everyone clapped, and Mattie smiled weakly. "And now

I'm going to call security. Maybe they'll believe that someone really is after Rick!" And with a toss of her pretty head, she stepped off the set, headed for the intercom behind the scenery.

"Well, dear, that's one way to meet a star," Lillian observed caustically, glaring at Nancy.

"Wait just a minute—" Nancy began. But then she decided it would be better not to say anything. Lillian might not be the friendliest person she'd ever met, but the last thing Nancy wanted was to make an enemy at the beginning.

Beginning of what? Nancy asked herself. An investigation? Was there really anything to investigate? After all, she reasoned, accidents do happen.

Dodging Lillian's pointed remark, Nancy excused herself and made her way over to the corner of the set. Rick was there, chatting with Bess.

"Ah, my savior!" he said when he saw Nancy. But her quick frown made it clear that she wasn't going to fall for his lines.

"Hey, girls," Rick suggested, "why don't the three of us go back to my dressing room? We can have a soda and get to know each other a little better while they're cleaning up this mess."

"Oh, we'd *love* to!" crooned Bess. Elbowing

Nancy in the ribs, she prompted her friend. "Wouldn't we?"

"I guess that would be all right," Nancy shrugged. Until security had finished looking around, no one would be allowed near the scene of the accident anyway. And maybe she could use the time to find out a little more about Rick Arlen.

"By the way, who was that woman—Lillian somebody—who was so angry at you earlier?" Nancy asked him as they headed down the empty corridor.

"Her name is Lillian Weiss," he hissed, making the name sound snakelike. "She's the assistant director. While Luther is up in the booth playing God, she's his watchdog."

"Sounds like she's not your favorite person."

"She's not. But then, Lillian's just a nobody around here. I don't let her get to me—she's not worth even thinking about."

Just then they came to a door with a polished brass star on it and Rick's name above the star. "Come into my parlor, said the spider to the fly," he quipped lightly. He ushered them in and closed the door quietly behind them.

The bright lights in the dressing room blinded Nancy for a moment when she stepped in.

"I love this room—it's so warm and bright. This is the place I go to get away from the craziness out there." He pointed toward the door. "Let's see, now," he mumbled. "I'd offer you a chocolate, but I'm afraid they're a little bitter. But can I get you something to drink?" Rick opened a small refrigerator.

Bess pushed a lock of blond hair behind her ear before she said, "Okay. Um, a diet soda for me."

"Pour vous?" he asked, turning to Nancy.

"The same, thanks."

"You're a very smart girl. And brave, too. Would you care to marry me?" Rick had taken Nancy's hand gently in his own, and now he offered her a bouquet of imaginary flowers with the other.

Nancy pulled her hand away and looked at him. "I have a boyfriend. Sorry," she said, apologizing.

"Ah—I'm crushed. Well, then," he purred, instantly turning to Bess and taking her hand. "How about you? Would you marry me?"

Bess's eyes twinkled mischievously. "Okay, you're on."

"Oh, you only like me for my looks," Rick complained. Nancy saw him catch a quick glimpse of himself in the mirror before he gazed back at Bess appreciatively. "But then, you're not too bad yourself."

Bess blushed. She seemed to melt into the dressing table as Rick stared at her.

Rick Arlen obviously knew how to flirt, Nancy observed. And Bess was definitely being taken in.

"Well," said Nancy, trying to break the spell, "for a guy who just barely escaped a terrible accident, you're in an incredibly good mood."

"Of course! Of course I am!" Rick said agreeably as he poured the sodas. "I was lucky. That's the best way to be if you're going to be in an accident. Don't you agree? But then, I've always been a lucky guy. I mean, I just met you two, didn't I?"

"Some people don't think the things that have been happening to you lately are accidents," Nancy said.

Rick sank into a plush chair and looked at her impatiently. "Some people are also frightened of their own shadows. Look, when you're a TV star, you have to expect a little craziness. It comes with the territory. Along with a lot of good things, too. Has anyone ever told you that you're beautiful," he added offhandedly to Bess. She almost swooned into his costume rack.

She's really eating this up, Nancy thought. Bess actually seemed to take Rick's baloney seriously.

"Look, I'd better get back to the set," Nancy said, putting down her soda. "Security should have had a good look around by now, and I want to find out exactly what happened. Are you coming, Bess?" she asked.

"Is it okay if I meet you back there in a little while?" Bess responded.

"Don't worry about Bess here," Rick put in with a grin. "I'll take care of her."

That was just what Nancy was afraid of.

Pushing through the thick, soundproof door, Nancy stepped back onto the set. Immediately she saw Mattie trying to break up a fight. One of the men was William Pappas. Nancy hadn't seen the other man before. He was slim, handsome, and at that moment his eyes were ablaze with anger.

"It was an accident!" Pappas was shouting. "Technicians are only human. Now, if you'll get off my back, I'll find out who was responsible and deal with that person. I can't do anything if you're going to stand here and scream at me all day!"

"You *still* don't get it, do you?" the other man shouted back. "Mattie could have been *killed* in there! And I promise you, if so much as a hair on my client's head is ever hurt, your network will be facing the biggest lawsuit the world has ever seen! Come on, Mattie!" He grabbed Mattie's arm and marched toward the door. Nancy ducked behind a piece of scenery and continued to watch.

"Dwayne, please, calm down!" Mattie protested. "No one was trying to hurt me! I was nowhere near the accident!"

"It's the network's responsibility to protect you from things like this, Mattie. Look at those shards of glass! What if one of them had cut your face? Your career would be ruined."

"Nobody is going to get hurt, Dwayne," Pappas said, calmer now. "This is never going to happen again. Now, will you please get out of here so we can clean up this mess and get on with the show?"

As Dwayne stalked off, Nancy heard Pappas remark to Mattie, "It's just my luck that that idiot agent was here today. The last thing I need is a nervous Nellie on the set the day the roof falls in. No offense, Mattie, but the man is a complete fool. Excuse me, please, will you?"

As Pappas breezed by her, Nancy grabbed Mattie's elbow, and they followed him. The producer walked immediately over to the chief of security and began asking questions. Nancy and Mattie got as close as they could without being noticed and listened intently.

"It looks like an accident, plain and simple, Mr. Pappas," the security man was saying.

"Thank you," Pappas muttered. Then he strode directly over to where the lighting technicians were gathered. "Which one of you was responsible for checking the lights this week?" he asked.

"I was," admitted one of the men unhappily. It was the man with the beard who had talked to Nancy and Bess earlier. "But they checked out fine. In fact, just this morning—"

"What's your name?" asked Pappas darkly.

"Uh, MacPherson, Mr. Pappas, but—"

"You're fired, MacPherson. Stop by the front office and pick up your severance pay. I don't ever want to see you around here again, understand?" Before the man could say another word, Pappas was gone.

Mattie and Nancy looked at each other. "You've got to believe me," Mattie whispered urgently. "That was no accident, I'm sure of it!"

Nancy sighed. If security thought it was an accident, it probably was. Still . . . "I think I'll take a look around myself. You never know."

There wasn't much to see. All the glass from the broken light had been swept into a pile in the corner, and the light itself was in pieces against the wall. Each piece had been tagged for reference. Security seemed to have done a thorough job.

Nancy was about to give up and go back to Rick's dressing room but decided to take a last look around. As she walked over to the back wall of the living room, a flash of something metallic caught her eye, and she bent to the floor. There, almost completely hidden from view, was a piece of metal with a bolt attached. One edge of the metal was shiny, as if it had been scraped or cut.

Nancy walked over to the lighting technician, who was gloomily gathering his things together. "Excuse me," she said, "but—could I ask you a question?"

The man turned around and looked at her for a moment. "Oh, hi, I remember you. You're the girl who saved Rick's life," he said with a smile. "I guess I should thank you. I'd have been in *real* trouble if he'd gotten hurt."

"You don't have to thank me," Nancy waved him off. "But you could tell me what this is." She showed him the bolt she'd found.

"Why, that's a C-clamp. They're used to hold the lights on the bar."

"Does it look odd to you? Is there anything strange about it?"

MacPherson studied the clamp briefly. "One end's been sawed," he gasped. "Almost clean through. The rest looks like it snapped off. This must be— But if—"

"Just what I was thinking," Nancy said, agreeing. "That was no accident this morning. The light was rigged so it would fall. Somebody tried to kill Rick Arlen—and almost succeeded!"

Chapter

Four

D O YOU BELIEVE me *now?*" Mattie was on the verge of tears as she pleaded with the chief of security. She and Nancy had just shown him the broken clamp. "I've been telling people for weeks that someone was after Rick, but nobody believed me. You've got to believe me now!"

"Now, Mattie," Pappas said, patting his leading lady on the arm. "Let's not get hysterical and blow this out of proportion."

"Well, I'll be," the security man muttered as he examined the C-clamp. "Where exactly did you say you found this, young lady?"

"By the back wall of the set," Nancy replied.

"Well, it proves the light was sabotaged. No doubt about it."

"This is just what I need," Pappas muttered in frustration. "I don't have enough problems without someone sabotaging my show!"

"Mr. Pappas, who actually has access to this stage?" the chief wanted to know.

"Well, the crew and the actors, of course. Nobody else, really. Maybe an occasional guest, but they all register at the front desk."

"Wasn't there a tour group in here earlier today?" Nancy asked.

Pappas snapped his fingers. "Right!"

"And some of them were mad at Rory Danner, too," Nancy said.

"You don't suppose some crazy fan could have—" Pappas shook his head.

"There're a lot of nuts out there, Mr. Pappas," the chief said. "All it takes is one person who can't tell fantasy from reality."

"That settles it!" Pappas exclaimed. "From now on this set is closed to anyone not directly involved in the show." Yelling across the studio, Pappas repeated his order for everyone to hear. "That means no guests, no agents, no mothers, fathers, sisters, or brothers. I want this set sealed tighter than a pharaoh's tomb!

"Now, we'll take a couple-hour break and then back to work. If you need anything, I'll be in my office."

After Pappas walked away, Nancy turned toward Mattie.

"Thank goodness he gave us a break," she told Nancy. "I've got to go rest." Rubbing her eyes, she added, "See you later. And thanks again for saving Rick's life." Flashing Nancy a grateful smile, Mattie walked off the set.

Since the set was closed to guests, Nancy and Bess had to leave. Nancy began to make her way back toward Rick's dressing room to collect Bess. But she soon realized she must have gone through the wrong door or made a wrong turn somewhere. One long corridor led to another, and for a moment Nancy didn't know which way to turn. Then the sound of a door slowly opening caught her attention. Instinctively knowing that she shouldn't be there, Nancy moved back into a recessed doorway and waited silently.

Nancy could just see Lillian Weiss nervously looking both ways before stepping into the hall. Once the door was closed behind her, Lillian seemed to relax. Nancy's heart was in her throat as she realized Lillian was heading straight for her. Nancy opened the door behind her and slammed it, making it sound as if she had just come through that door. She stepped out into the corridor.

"Well, well," Lillian said, greeting Nancy with a snarl. "Is our fair rescuer lost and helpless?"

"Yes, I guess I am. I was looking for Rick's dressing room, actually," Nancy told her. Well, it was almost the truth.

"Continue down this corridor and make your first left," Lillian snapped. "And by the way, it was nice knowing you. I'm sure now that Pappas has closed the set, you won't be around anymore. Too bad. I'm sure you were Rick's favorite little bodyguard." With a smug smile, Lillian continued down the hall and disappeared around a corner.

The room that Lillian had come out of turned out to be the prop room. After making sure she was alone, Nancy ventured inside.

At first she was overwhelmed by what she saw. The room was huge, with several long aisles. Stacked from floor to ceiling, making an incredible clutter, were thousands upon thousands of items—anything that could ever possibly be needed on the set of the show. As organized as the room seemed to be, with everything numbered and labeled, there was no way to keep it all neat. Dust covered some of the items that hadn't been used recently, and Nancy felt her nose begin to itch.

There seemed to be nobody there, but when Nancy sneezed, she heard a rustling in a far corner. A copy of the *Daily News* moved, and a grizzled head poked out from under it. The old man had a mop of unruly white hair flowing out from an ancient orange cap.

"Who's there?" a crackly voice called. "I'm awake, I'm awake. On the job all the time, yessir! What can I do for you?"

Nancy couldn't help smiling at the wizened old man. He wore red suspenders, which held up a pair of baggy gray pants, and he was covered with as much dust as everything else in the room. Nancy would have almost believed that he had been sleeping there uninterrupted for years.

"Sorry, I must have opened the wrong door," she said, apologizing.

"Oh, it's good to have a little company," the man said. "This week has been just kitchen stuff and living room knickknacks, day after day. I've been sitting here reading my paper all week without seeing a soul."

"But wasn't the assistant director in here just a moment ago?" Nancy said.

"Who? Lillian? Nah, haven't seen Lillian in ages. The only time she ever came into the prop room was to complain that a butcher knife didn't look sharp enough. I had to put a little oil on it to give it that threatening gleam when the camera panned in on it. That's an old prop man's trick, you know."

"Achoo!" Nancy couldn't help sneezing again. "Are you sure no one was in here earlier?" she asked again, persisting.

"Absolutely one hundred percent, young lady. And nobody gets anything by me."

That's what you think, Nancy thought as she said goodbye to the prop man. As she stepped back into the corridor and made her way to Rick's dressing room, Nancy's mind was in a whirl. Maybe one of the fans from the tour group *had* tampered with the klieg light. She supposed it was possible. But even so, something funny was definitely going on. What had Lillian been doing in the prop room? And why was she so hostile? Nancy was determined to find out. And that meant she had to get onto the set again the next day and do some more checking around.

Here I am, she said to herself as she turned a corner and saw the familiar door with the star on it. Wait till I tell Bess what I found!

A moment later, after a quick knock, she threw open the door, smiling broadly. What she saw made her stop dead. Bess was in Rick's arms, and they looked about a split second away from a kiss too steamy for TV!

Chapter

Five

N ancy!" Bess cried, awkwardly trying to disentangle herself from Rick's embrace.

Nancy looked from a blushing Bess to Rick and back, "I'm sorry to interrupt, but—"

"It's not what you think!" Bess said, interrupting her as she tossed her blond hair over her shoulder and straightened her collar. "Rick just asked me to help him rehearse, that's all."

"She's very talented," Rick said, putting his arm around Bess's waist and drawing her closer.

"Well, I just came to tell you that Pappas

closed the set to all visitors," Nancy said, looking at Bess.

But Bess wasn't about to let anything ruin her day. "Nancy, you'll never guess what Rick has offered to do!"

"It's really nothing," Rick said, protesting.

"Nothing?" Bess replied, her eyes dancing with excitement. "You call taking me all over the city in a limousine nothing?"

"Well, I already have the limousine." Rick shrugged modestly.

"He's going to give me a personal tour of the city on Saturday! Would you believe he's never been on top of the Empire State Building?"

"How can you live in New York and not visit the Empire State Building?" Nancy asked.

"Actually, a lot of New Yorkers have never been there," he explained. "We always say we're going to go someday, but somehow we never get around to it. It'll be a real treat for me."

Bess continued to gaze at the handsome TV star. Nancy couldn't help worrying that her friend might be getting in over her head.

"Bess, aren't you forgetting that Rick might be in danger? I don't know if it's such a great idea for you to be alone with him, you know."

"Don't be silly!" Rick laughed, wiping his makeup off with a thick cloth. "I can take care of both of us. Listen, I've got an even better idea—why don't you come, too? I'm sure I could round up a friend for you."

"That's great!" Bess cried happily, turning to Nancy.

"Okay, count me in," Nancy agreed. Spending the day with Rick was one way to keep an eye on him. And on Bess.

"Come on, Bess," she said, taking her friend by the elbow. "We'd better leave the set. Nice meeting you, Rick." Nancy turned to the door, but Bess wasn't quite finished talking to Rick.

"Well, I'm sorry we have to go so soon, but we're definitely on for Saturday, aren't we?" she asked.

"I can hardly wait, love," he replied, blowing her a kiss. "Till then, 'Parting is such sweet sorrow.'"

As soon as she closed the door, Bess stood stock-still for a moment. Then she leaned on the wall in a daze. "Did you hear? He called me 'love.'"

"I heard," Nancy replied uneasily.

"Oh, Nancy," Bess cooed, "he's so wonderful! Not at all conceited like some big stars probably are. Just think, I have a date with *the* Rick Arlen. Me—Bess Marvin, regular person! Do you know how many girls would kill for a date with the star of 'Danner's Dream'?"

"Yeah—" Nancy said, only half paying attention. She was wondering who was trying to kill Rick Arlen—and why?

"We were standing there, watching this intense scene. I mean, it was so quiet you could hear your heart beating!" Bess was going over the whole day as Nancy's aunt emptied a package of white mushrooms into her food processor. "And then, well, the light just snapped! Right in front of our eyes! Right, Nancy?"

Nancy looked up from the microwave, where she was getting ready to bake three potatoes. "Uh-huh," she agreed.

"And Nancy saved the day. You should have seen her," Bess said, continuing. "I don't know how she reacted so fast. The light only missed him by a few inches. And Rick is amazing. He wasn't even afraid! He said it was all in a day's work. Can you believe it?"

Eloise's eyes clouded over with worry. "I'm not sure I want you two poking around in a place where they have accidents like that," she said, shaking her head.

Nancy looked over at Bess and put her finger on her lips, but Bess didn't pick up on it.

"Oh, no!" Bess went on. "It *wasn't* an accident! Nancy found the evidence—somebody tampered with the light!"

"Nancy!" Aunt Eloise exclaimed. "Do you mean to say Mattie was right to suspect something was wrong? Oh, dear, please be careful! I don't want you getting hurt."

Bess laughed and shook her head. "Don't worry, Rick says it's just some crazy fan trying to scare him. Now that they've closed the set, I'm sure there won't be any more trouble."

Just then the phone rang.

"Hello?" Eloise answered. "Oh, yes, Mattie, we're here. Come on up." Replacing the receiver, she said, "I hope it's all right if Mattie joins us. I should have asked you first."

"It's fine with me!" Bess cried happily.

Nancy went to the vegetable bin and took out another potato. After rinsing it, she popped it into the microwave.

"That's it," Eloise said. "Dinner in ten minutes."

In a few minutes there was a knock on the door, and Nancy went to open it.

"Hi, everybody!" Mattie called as she breezed into the apartment with a bouquet of spring flowers. Nancy was amazed at how carefree Mattie seemed. "Oh, I'm so happy you're on the case," she cried, embracing Nancy warmly. "I know nothing bad can happen to Rick now."

Nancy frowned slightly. Everyone seemed to think Rick Arlen was safe, including Rick himself. She wasn't at all convinced.

"Did you hear about your niece, this morning's heroine?" Mattie said, going over to kiss

Eloise and hand her the flowers. "You weren't exaggerating when you told me how brave she was."

Eloise reddened and looked over at Nancy. "Don't get the wrong idea," she warned. "I'm proud of you, but that doesn't mean I approve of your taking unnecessary risks. Please be careful."

"I will," Nancy promised.

Dinner was ready, and the four of them gathered around the large oak table in the dining area.

"Marinated steak. Smells great, and I don't mind saying so myself," Eloise remarked. "I may not be the greatest cook, but every once in a while I do all right."

"I can testify personally that she's a fantastic cook," Mattie said with a laugh. After they ate and chatted for a while, Mattie turned more serious and asked, "So, Nancy, what do you think? Was it someone from the tour group who tampered with the light?"

"Well, some people seem to think that," Nancy answered. "But from what I can tell, his fans aren't the only ones who're angry at Rick. There are other people—people who see him every day. Pappas, for instance. Or Lillian Weiss. Maybe others, too."

"Hah! You don't know the half of it," Mattie said. "There isn't a person on that set who Rick hasn't alienated at one time or another."

"Really? Why?" Nancy wondered.

"Oh, Rick's just— He's talented, handsome, and rich. Some people would hate him just for that, but he's also walked over a lot of people to get where he is. He's used a lot of people, broken a lot of hearts—" She sighed deeply.

Was one of those broken hearts Mattie's? Nancy wondered. The actress seemed so fragile and sad when she talked about Rick.

"I wish I could point to just one person and say, 'That's the one,' but Rick has made a lot of enemies." Mattie shook her head and reached for her glass of mineral water.

"People resent his success," Bess commented. "He was telling me about that today, about how jealous people are of him. How they all want something from him."

"Oh," Mattie said, turning to face Bess. "You two were talking together?"

"Uh-huh!" Bess said happily. "We found out we have a lot in common."

"I see," Mattie said, looking down at her plate.

"Wait a minute," Bess said slowly. "You two aren't going out or anything, are you?"

"Oh, no," Mattie quickly replied. "That is, not anymore."

So, Mattie *was* one of those broken hearts! Nancy thought.

"Oh, phew." Bess breathed a sigh of relief.

"I wouldn't want to steal somebody else's boyfriend or anything. You see, he's asked me out for Saturday."

"He—he asked you out?" Mattie whispered. Her eyes grew incredibly wide, and her mouth fell open.

"Yes," Nancy interjected soothingly. "And I'm going along, too. It's perfect, don't you think? That way I can keep an eye on Rick."

"I see." Mattie looked somewhat calmed by Nancy's explanation. Still, she turned to Bess with a sudden, compelling stare. "Just be careful, please," she said, warning her. "You don't know Rick the way I do—you don't know how dangerous he can be."

Chapter

Six

LISTEN, BESS—" MATTIE relaxed her stare a bit, trying hard not to look so severe. "I really don't want to upset you, but, honestly, Rick can really love them and leave them. Maybe it's because deep down inside, he's very unsure of himself. Or maybe he's become too successful too fast, and— Sometimes I wonder if he can really handle it."

"Rick? Unsure of himself?" Bess shook her head in disbelief. "I'm sorry, Mattie. I don't think you know the real Rick."

"Maybe not, but I've known him a long time. We did summer stock together years ago.

He was different then, warm and sincere. In the past few years, he's really changed. He can be so cold now, even cruel."

"Well, maybe he just hasn't met the right girl yet," Bess suggested.

"Wait a minute," Nancy interrupted. "Mattie, why are you so concerned about a man you've just told us is cold, cruel, and steps on people?"

"Oh, I don't know," Mattie answered softly. "I guess I still think of him as a friend, even if it didn't work out between us." Looking over at Nancy imploringly, she added, "Rick would never admit it, but I'm sure that way down deep he's scared. I'd just feel so much better if you were on the set tomorrow."

Bess rolled her eyes and got up from the table. Nancy watched her go. She hoped Bess knew what she was doing where Rick was concerned.

"I'd like to be there myself," Nancy replied, turning back to Mattie. "But now that the set's closed to visitors—"

"Wait a minute!" Mattie cried. Her eyes shimmered with excitement. "I just got a brilliant idea! We're shooting a hospital scene tomorrow, and I'll bet I could get you and Bess jobs as extras! What do you think? Will you do it?"

Across the kitchen, Bess couldn't help jumping up and down with excitement. "That would be fantastic!"

Nancy thought for a moment. "Are you sure you could do it?"

"Almost sure. Here, let me call the casting director. Eloise, do you have a phone book handy?"

Nancy's aunt brought the book over as Bess loaded the dishwasher. "Just imagine, Nancy, appearing on my favorite soap!"

"We're in luck!" Mattie announced, hanging up the phone a few minutes later. "She says you two can be nurses. Just report to the studio at seven sharp, and go straight to the costume room as soon as you get there."

"But what if people recognize us?" Nancy wondered out loud.

"Oh, they won't recognize you." Mattie laughed and stood up to leave. "No one ever looks at the extras. Besides, when you're on camera you'll probably have wigs and uniforms on. You probably won't even recognize yourselves."

"You know, Nancy," Bess said after Mattie had gone. "No matter what anyone says, I've read that a lot of big stars started out as extras. You never know—this could be my lucky break!"

Bess and Nancy had reported to the studio at seven the next morning. After the dry blocking, in which they learned what they were to do, they reported to makeup and wardrobe. Now, standing on pedestals as two wardrobe people finished their final fittings for the dress rehearsal, Bess and Nancy couldn't help giggling.

"You're really a knockout as a brunette, Nancy!" Bess said.

Nancy looked over at her friend, who was wearing an identical uniform. She had a white nurse's cap over her bright red wig, and Nancy had never seen her look more excited.

"Your dress rehearsal will be third, ladies," a production assistant told them. "After the big love scene, which is the second, report to Lillian. You know where to stand and what to do from the first rehearsal. So, break a leg. Oh, if you want to catch Rick and Mattie in rehearsal, you can. Rory and Serena are going to have a big scene. It's supposed to be pretty hot stuff."

Bess immediately dashed down the corridor to the set, determined not to miss a word of Mattie and Rick's scene. It was all Nancy could do to keep up with her.

Watching the cast and crew gather around the set of Serena Livingstone's living room, Nancy could feel their edginess. The near-disaster of the day before had obviously gotten to everyone. Even though the set was closed to outsiders, Nancy could tell that nobody felt truly safe.

The only person who seemed at ease was Rick. Flashing a smile at Bess as he walked onto the set, he looked as if he were on top of the world.

He took his place in the middle of the set, and slowly Rick Arlen seemed to fade away. When the director finally called "Action," he had become Rory Danner.

In the scene, Rory was supposed to tell Serena that he'd be hers forever, if she would have him. Even though it was an intense scene, Nancy noticed that Rick was reading nearly all his lines from the teleprompter. But then, with all the excitement the day before, she reasoned, he probably hadn't had time to memorize them.

Mattie was having trouble with her lines, too. She had excused herself early the night before to go home and work, but obviously she didn't remember much. Although she was really throwing herself into the scene, Nancy noticed that she, too, kept glancing over at her teleprompter to check her lines.

"Should I leave, Serena? Is that what you want?" Rick asked, pacing in front of Mattie nervously.

"No, Rory, don't go. I love you," Serena said. Her voice was quivering, and her emerald eyes were full of tears. "I've always loved you, even when you didn't want me."

"Cut!" came the director's voice. "Mattie, I need you to cool it a little. If you start the scene at such a high emotional pitch, we won't have anywhere to go."

"Right, Luther." Mattie nodded up to the director's booth.

"Okay, everyone, take it from 'Should I leave,'" Lillian ordered.

"Should I leave, Serena? Is that what you want?" Rick said.

"No, Rory, don't go. I love you! I've always loved you, even when you didn't want me."

They were into it by then. Mattie and Rick were utterly convincing, making everyone who was watching really believe they were desperately in love. Bess had tears in her eyes as she watched them move slowly toward each other. Finally, Serena collapsed in Rory's arms.

"Here comes her big speech," Lillian muttered under her breath to nobody in particular. "Watch her screw it up."

"Oh, Rory, I want to do so many things with you," Mattie whispered hoarsely. "I want to take walks in the rain with you, I want to sit with you under the stars on a deserted beach. I want to dance with you, to sing with you, to—"

Mattie suddenly fell silent. She stood as if frozen, her eyes fixed on the teleprompter, her beautiful face a terrible white. Then, as everyone looked on in horror, she let out a blood-curdling scream and slumped slowly to the floor.

Chapter

Seven

"MATTIE! MATTIE!"

"What happened?"

"Is she all right?"

"Don't touch her!"

Everyone gathered around Mattie, who was lying on the floor. After what seemed forever, her eyes began to flutter open. She looked dazed. Mattie struggled to her feet with Rick's help. The look in her eyes only grew wilder.

"Look!" she cried, pointing to the teleprompter.

Her monologue had been changed. It read: "I WANT TO DANCE WITH YOU, TO SING WITH YOU,

TO MURDER YOU. YES, YOUR TIME IS UP, RICK ARLEN. I'M GOING TO KILL YOU. I'M GOING TO WATCH YOU DIE A HORRIBLE DEATH, AND I'M GOING TO LAUGH."

"What in the name of— What is this?" Pappas yelled. "Get me the teleprompter operator! I want to talk to her right now!"

"I'm here, Mr. Pappas." A short red-haired girl spoke up.

"Would you care to explain this?" he asked, arching his eyebrows.

"Well, sir, I, uh—I really can't explain it," the girl stammered. "I got here early to type in the scene, and I was at the keyboard all morning. The only time I left was to take a phone call. And I know I wasn't gone for more than a minute because when I picked up the phone, there was no one there. I—I didn't think—"

"Exactly, you didn't think." Pappas shot the operator a harsh look. "You're fired. And whoever's job it was to keep strangers off this set, you're fired, too." Then, to the frightened cast and crew he said, "I'll fire every last one of you if I have to. This nonsense has got to stop!"

Nancy watched the producer from the sidelines. He seemed genuinely concerned, but what if it was all an act? What if beneath all his theatrics, there was something completely different going on, something much more calculated—and sinister?

She noticed Lillian Weiss, too. Lillian was off in a corner, trying to be inconspicuous, but nothing could hide the pleased look on her face. She was loving every minute of all this.

"Okay, everybody," Luther's voice boomed from the director's booth. "Lunch break. And when we come back, let's try to get this show back on schedule, shall we?"

"Calm down, Mattie! You're not going to let some practical joker ruin your day, are you?" Rick opened the front door of the studio for them, and Mattie, Bess, and Nancy filed past him onto the sidewalk.

"Come on," he added with a grin. "Let me treat you all to lunch—while I'm still alive, that is."

"Stop it! Stop pretending everything's fine!" Mattie turned on him, her green eyes flashing. "You've got to be terrified! Why don't you just come out and admit it?"

"Me? Terrified? Don't be ridiculous—they can't kill me. The world needs me! Besides, it'd spoil the ratings if I died."

"Oh, I could just punch you," Mattie growled. "And I'll pay for my own lunch, thank you."

"Whatever you say." Rick shrugged. "I'll just have to treat Bess—and Nancy, of course. Right, ladies?"

Bess and Nancy said nothing, embarrassed

by the way Rick was taunting Mattie. Nancy started to walk off by herself.

"Hey, look who's here!" said Rick, his attention caught by a man at the studio door. "It's the president of the losers' league himself. Hi, Dwayne."

Dwayne Casper, Mattie's agent, rushed up to them, pointedly ignoring Rick's remark. Nancy stopped and observed the scene at a short distance from the others. "Mattie!" he cried, throwing his arms around her. "I was bringing some of your new head shots to the front office and I heard what happened. It's absolutely outrageous! Are you all right, darling?"

"Oh, I suppose so," Mattie replied softly, shaking free of his embrace. "It was awfully upsetting, but—"

"But nothing," Dwayne said, interrupting. "You're in danger, and I won't have it!"

"Keep your shirt on, Casper," Rick said, with a scornful laugh. "This nut is supposedly after me, not Mattie. Why don't you leave us alone and go hover over some of your other clients. If you have any, that is."

"Rick!" Mattie cried sharply.

"It's all right, Mattie, he doesn't bother me. As long as you're all right—"

"I'm fine, Dwayne. Please don't worry about me." Mattie smiled at him warmly. "Honest."

"Yeah, don't worry, old buddy. I'll take care of Mattie," Rick said, trying to assure him.

"Oh, I'm sure you will." Dwayne sneered. Then he turned to Mattie and took her by the hand, looking deeply into her eyes. "I want you to promise to call me if there's any more trouble on the set."

Mattie nodded, then Dwayne walked off, throwing a nasty look over his shoulder at Rick.

"For pete's sake, Mattie," Rick muttered before Dwayne was out of earshot, "when are you going to dump that jerk and get yourself a real agent!"

"Oh, Dwayne's not so bad," Mattie answered, watching the man disappear. "Remember, he took me on as a client when nobody else would even give me an interview."

"But you've come a long way since then. You're a star now. You should have a major agency representing you," he said as they started walking to catch up with Nancy.

"I don't know. Somehow I'd feel like a rat if I left Dwayne."

"All I know is, a major agency could get you a lot more work and more money. And a girl with your talent deserves the best." Seeing he was getting nowhere, Rick threw up his hands. "All right, I won't say another word. You know how I feel, though." He stopped in front of an expensive-looking restaurant. "Here we are. Serena, Nurse Sanford, Nurse Johnson, would you care to have lunch with me?" he said, opening the restaurant door for them.

"It's Saturday morning and time for another edition of 'Soap Opera Weekly,' where we bring you the latest on your favorite shows and introduce you to the stars," the television announcer was saying as Bess shook Nancy's shoulder.

"Wake up, Nancy Drew!" Bess said, mimicking the announcer. "Come on. The alarm went off ten minutes ago! Your aunt's still sleeping so I wheeled the TV in here. Rick's going to be on 'Soap Opera Weekly' this morning. We can watch while we get dressed."

"Mumpfh—" Nancy mumbled, burying her head under the pillow. Was it really morning already?

She and Bess and her aunt Eloise had had such a great time the night before. They'd gone to see *Soft Shoe*, the Broadway musical smash of the season. The show was wonderful, but they'd stopped for a bite to eat afterward. By the time they got home, it was almost one in the morning.

Flipping over and squinting at the TV, Nancy saw shots of different soap opera stars as the upbeat theme song played in the background.

"Our special 'Soap Opera Weekly' guest today is the star of 'Danner's Dream'!" the announcer said. "Will he and Serena Livingstone finally tie the knot this time? Mr. Sex Appeal himself, Rick Arlen, will be here with us in just a few minutes! But first—"

The commercial came on, and Nancy realized there was no way she was going to get back to sleep. Not with Bess rummaging around the room, tossing one outfit after another on the bed and saying things like, "What do you think, Nancy? The pink or the yellow?"

Pulling herself up onto her elbows, Nancy yawned and looked out the window. It was a glorious day outside—warm and sunny. A perfect day for seeing the sights, she thought happily.

"He's on! He's on!" Bess shouted a few minutes later. Nancy turned from the closet and saw Rick. He was seated casually across from the interviewer, waving and nodding as the audience clapped and cheered.

Cleverly refusing to give away any of the show's carefully guarded secrets, Rick did admit that he was considering leaving the show at the end of the season to star in a movie. The audience groaned, then applauded.

"Tell us about the real Rick Arlen," the interviewer prompted. "Could we be hearing wedding bells soon?"

Laughing, Rick made an old joke about the gossip columns having him engaged to three different girls. "But then, you never can tell," he added slyly, blowing a kiss to a "special lady out there."

"He means me!" Bess cried happily.

"I don't think so. That's just talk, Bess. He could mean anybody—or nobody."

Bess shot her friend an angry scowl, and Nancy decided to back off.

After the interview with Rick, the show moved on to an update of that network's daytime and evening soap operas. Bess snapped the TV off then.

"He said he'd be here in an hour. I can't wait!" Bess scooped up her makeup and headed for the bathroom. "Hey, I wonder who he'll bring for you, Nancy. I mean, any friend of Rick's is probably cute, but I wonder what he'll be like."

An hour later the apartment intercom buzzed, signaling the arrival of Rick and his limousine.

Bess checked herself in the mirror one last time. She looked terrific in an oversize cotton cardigan and flowing skirt and flats. "Not bad," she pronounced. "Come on, Nancy!" With that, she flew down the steps of the brownstone to the waiting limousine.

"Not bad at all," Nancy admitted, looking admiringly at Rick's limo. The uniformed driver ushered them into the backseat, where Rick was waiting.

"Good morning, girls!" he said brightly. "Welcome to my abode on the road."

The first order of business was to pick up Rick's friend, a guy named Gilbert Frost. "He's an old pal from acting school," Rick explained. "You'll love him."

Bess threw Nancy a meaningful look, but Nancy just sighed and looked out the window. There was no way that she was going to fall for any of Rick Arlen's friends—not when she was in love with Ned Nickerson. Of course, Ned would understand her being on this date —she had to go. Someone's life was in jeopardy.

At the corner of Twenty-third Street and Park Avenue South, she noticed a skinny guy in jeans and running shoes, leaning against a streetlight. He looked totally normal, except that he was wearing big black-rimmed glasses and a false nose.

"What?" Nancy mumbled as the limo stopped in front of him. The man swept down in a low courtly bow.

"Hey there, Gil!" Rick laughed, opening the door. "Girls, I'd like you to meet Gilbert Frost. Say hello, Gilbert."

"Hello, Gilbert!" the guy mimicked, sliding into the plush limo.

Bess was giggling uncontrollably, and Nancy

couldn't help smiling as Rick's friend took off his glasses, revealing another pair underneath.

Finally, they pulled back into traffic and Nancy got a good look at Gilbert. Without his getup on, he was pretty cute. He had glossy black hair and warm brown eyes that twinkled with laughter.

"Gil is going to be the next host at the Comedy Basement," Rick said. "He does stand-up."

"I also do sit up and grow up," Gil announced. Everyone groaned.

Throwing a proprietary arm around Bess's shoulder, Rick instructed the driver to take them to Forty-second Street and the Hudson River.

"Today we're going to do all those corny things you see in old movies about New York," Rick said. "Like go on a boat trip around Manhattan and to the top of the Empire State Building. Bess is a very old-fashioned girl," he explained to his friend.

"Rick Arlen! I am *not!*" Bess protested. Secretly, though, she was flattered by his remark.

By the time they got to the West Side pier, the four of them were relaxed and having a great time. Before leaving the limo, Rick put on sunglasses and an old hat. That way, most of his face was covered. "Just normal precautions," he insisted. "These go everywhere with me. Otherwise, the fans—well, I'm sure you can imagine."

"I think you look adorable like that," Gilbert said. Rick punched his friend lightly on the arm, and they all piled out of the car.

"So, Gil, how did you get involved in show business?" Nancy asked while they waited on deck for the cruise to start.

"Oh, now we're going way back—to the day little Freddie Gilbert was born in Illinois in a log cabin— No, no, just kidding. How did I get involved in show business, you ask. Thank goodness someone cares besides my mother."

In spite of his nonstop chatter and putdown humor, Nancy decided she liked Gil. He seemed a little lonely, somehow, and afraid to be just himself, but instinct told her he had a good heart.

"You see, my real name is Fred Gilbert. I had to change it after I got to New York. There already was a Fred Gilbert out there in the show business stratosphere. And so Gilbert Frost was born. But he had the wrong nose. So I changed that, too. And then I had to darken my hair. By the time I was finished, the same club owners who used to tell me to get lost were dying to sign me. What can I tell you? It's a crazy business. Maybe someday I'll even make enough to pay my rent. And if I'm really lucky, I might even hit it big like old Rick here."

"I'm sure you will," Nancy said, looking up.

The view from the boat was spectacular —the skyline sparkled in the noon sun.

But as the boat trip continued and they finally circled the northern tip of Manhattan, Nancy couldn't help feeling that something was wrong. All through the ride, she had been keeping an eye on Rick. And she noticed other people were watching him, too. Nancy saw two women look at him, jab each other, and whisper. And a child tugged on his father's sleeve and pointed toward Rick. A portly man was also watching him, although he pretended to be looking at something else.

As the boat swung into the final leg of the tour, Nancy recognized the portly man. He had been the one cursing Rory Danner on the tour of the set just two days before.

"Attention, ladies and gentlemen. We will be docking in a few minutes. Please disembark via the white stairs on the port side of the boat. That's the left, to all you landlubbers," the tour guide instructed.

"That's him! That's Rick Arlen!" a young woman suddenly shrieked.

An excited murmur went through the crowd, and everyone turned to look at Rick.

"Take the hat off, Rory! We know it's you!" a woman called out good-naturedly. The group laughed, and Rick cooperated.

"Ah, my fans." He smiled and waved.

"You're the greatest—all of you! I love you madly!"

"Rick, may I have your autograph?" a woman cried happily. Everyone crowded around him and began rifling through their bags for pens, too.

"Write one for my niece, Rick!"

"Oh, Mr. Arlen, thank you!"

Rick was standing by the guardrail signing the backs of envelopes, napkins, address books, and matchbook covers. Suddenly, the man who had been on the studio tour lunged forward, his eyes wild, his voice like thunder. "You killed Jill Rowan, and now you want to destroy Serena Livingstone. Well, I won't let you! I'm not going to let filth like you near her! You're going to die, Rory Danner—right now!"

With that, the man lunged for Rick, sending him halfway over the rail. He was about to plunge into the river!

Chapter
Eight

LEAPING FOR RICK, Nancy and Gilbert grabbed him just in time and pulled him safely back over the rail. Nancy felt a pair of hamlike hands on her shoulders. She turned to face the assailant and delivered a swift kick to his left shin. Then she seized his hand and flipped him head over heels onto the deck. The ship's crew then held him pinned against the deck until the ship had docked and the police arrived, followed by a couple of reporters.

"Okay, fella, let's go," a police officer said, leading the man to a patrol car. "You'll feel a lot better after a nice long rest."

"I killed Rory Danner and the world will be a better place for it!" the man exclaimed. "He was filth! Filth!"

"Sure, sure," another police officer said, agreeing. "You can tell the doctor all about it."

As their limo pulled out of the parking lot, the crowd cheered Rick. He was leaning out the window, smiling and waving.

"Thank you, everyone!" he called. He slipped back into the car. "Well, thank goodness that's over. And thank you, Gil. And Nancy." Turning to Bess, he added, "You certainly know how to pick your friends, love."

Gil still seemed a bit shaken. "You know, Rick, the way you were hanging over the edge there, I thought you were history." He shuddered. "I'm going to sign up for karate lessons next week. I want to be prepared for fame."

"Let's just put the whole thing behind us, okay? Now it's time to celebrate!" Rick grinned devilishly. "Why not go for the best! Driver—take us to Trump Tower!"

Later, riding up the escalator from the lobby of the brass-and-marble palace, Bess and Nancy looked around in wonder. The place was amazing!

"This makes the River Heights mall look

like a mom-and-pop store," Nancy whispered. She looked all around her as they rose ever higher through the glittering atrium.

"Tell me about it!" Bess said enthusiastically. "Rick, I can't believe people actually *live* in this building."

"They do," he assured her. "There are apartments here that sell for millions."

"Seriously?" Bess couldn't believe it. "What do they have, solid gold faucets?"

"Almost," Gil replied. "You'd be amazed at what people spend their money on."

"Cappuccino, anyone?" Rick broke in cheerfully. They had just come to an attractive café on an upper level.

Soon they were all sitting around a table sipping cups of the strong Italian coffee.

"You know what being here makes me realize?" Bess was saying. "I've realized that I'd make a great millionaire."

"I think you'd make a lovely one, too," Rick said, flirting. "In fact, I saw something in a shop across the way that I think you should have. Be right back."

A minute later Rick came back to the table, holding a silk scarf printed in pastel geometric shapes. It matched Bess's outfit perfectly.

"Oh, Rick!" she exclaimed. "It's beautiful!"

"Wear it and think of me," he murmured. "So, everyone, are you ready to scale the heights? It's such a clear beautiful day—what do you say we catch the view from the Empire State Building?"

"Sounds great!" Bess was beaming. Anything Rick said would have sounded great to her.

"I used to sell souvenirs at the observatory," Gil threw in. "That was when I still *worked* for a living." He straightened up and helped Nancy from her chair. "Madame?" he said. "Your chariot awaits. That is, *Rick's* chariot awaits," he said, correcting himself.

By the time they reached Thirty-fourth Street and made their way up to the top, the sun had slipped much closer to the horizon. Rick and Bess, their arms around each other's waists, stood at the observatory's edge, gazing into the distance. Gil had stopped to chat with his old coworkers at the souvenir shop, so Nancy wandered off by herself.

Up that high, the wind cut like a knife, seeming to come from all directions. It blew Nancy's hair wildly around her as she stared down at the magical city. The noise from the street sounded like a low moan up there, almost human and full of sadness. It made Nancy shudder for a moment.

As she looked out over the city below her, she felt a growing sense of dread. The police had arrested the deranged fan that afternoon, but she was still worried. In the late afternoon sun, Nancy had a sudden, powerful feeling that someone *else* was after Rick. Someone who was not only crazy, but also clever, determined, and deadly. Nancy felt an icy shiver go through her. Someone was waiting down on the street—she was sure of it—waiting to end Rick Arlen's life.

Bess scooped up one last mouthful of chocolate mousse pie and sighed contentedly. "What a dinner! I'm in heaven."

"Not bad," Gil agreed, glancing around at the glass walls of Tavern on the Green. Positioned on the edge of Central Park, the view out the windows of the restaurant was of trees decorated with tiny white lights. The park looked like an enchanted fairyland, in direct contrast to the city around it.

When the check came, Rick picked it up. "What's money for if not to treat friends?" he asked, placing a gold credit card on the small black lacquered tray the waiter had brought.

"What a day!" Bess remarked happily. "What a night, too! I've had such a fabulous time today, Rick . . . thanks to you."

Rick looked genuinely pleased as he took her hand in his. "There's just one more thing I'd like to do. I could use a little exercise after this dinner, and it's such a great night—why don't we take a walk beside the park?"

Bess's eyes were twinkling with delight. Rick

seemed to be having a hard time saying good night to her!

"A walk sounds wonderful," Nancy said.

"Good, we're on!" Gil agreed.

Stepping out onto the sidewalk along the park, Rick and Bess linked arms. They were completely caught up in each other as they giggled and joked, walking ahead of the other two. Nancy watched them carefully as she half listened to Gil, who was telling her the rest of his life story.

"Then I realized I had to change my material," he was saying. "Nobody goes for rubber-chicken jokes anymore. So I began writing myself a whole new act. . . ."

Nancy couldn't help worrying about Bess. She was heading for trouble, Nancy was sure of that. Even if Rick was sincere, how could it last? They lived miles from each other. And a broken heart was the last thing Bess needed.

The sound of a speeding car made Nancy spin around. A taxicab jumped its lane and screeched diagonally across the street. Suddenly a broken heart was the least of Bess's troubles. The out-of-control cab was headed onto the sidewalk, aimed straight at Rick —and Bess!

Chapter

Nine

WATCH OUT!" NANCY screamed. Racing up to pull Bess away from the oncoming taxi, she managed to get just close enough to grab her friend's arm as the taxi swerved onto the sidewalk. It barely missed the stunned Bess before jumping the curb back onto the street and careening away.

Bess stood absolutely still in the middle of the sidewalk. "Nancy? Am I okay?" she asked in a dazed voice.

"Your shirt is torn, but I think you're fine."

Suddenly Bess looked around frantically. "Rick! Where's Rick?"

"Right here," he answered. They all turned

and saw Rick's head poking out from behind a tree. "See? I told you it would take a silver bullet to get me! Not even a scratch," he added, proudly showing them his arms and legs.

"Don't tell m-me that was just an accident," Gil stammered, running a hand nervously through his hair. "He never even hit the brakes."

"He's right, Rick." Bess seemed quite shaken now. "Maybe there's more than one crazy fan after you."

Nancy bit her lip and thought for a moment. This latest incident confirmed her worst fears. She knew now that the crude attempt on Rick's life on the boat trip was just a sideshow. The main event was still to come.

Gil was still shaking. "Well, I don't know about you folks," he said, "but I've had about all the excitement I can take for one day. Next time we get together, Rick, remind me to take out extra insurance."

"Hey, calm down. It's the price of life in the fast lane, that's all." Rick laughed nervously. "Come on, I'll give you a lift home on my way downtown. Bess?" Turning to Bess, he pulled her gently to him and gave her a lingering kiss.

They walked back to the limo, and Nancy and Gil climbed in. Nancy turned her head away, embarrassed, while Bess and Rick stood on the sidewalk. They were whispering, probably about what had just happened.

Nancy frowned. Things looked bad, very bad indeed. It was as if Bess hadn't even noticed that she and Rick had almost been killed!

"It's just a feeling I get, Ned, but it's a strong one. Something's very wrong here." Nancy flung herself down on the dark blue sofa and filled her boyfriend, Ned Nickerson, in on everything that had happened since she'd arrived in New York. "I only wish you weren't so far away." She sighed wistfully.

"Same here," Ned agreed. "I miss you."

"I miss you, too. And I could really use your help on this case."

"Can I do anything from here?"

"Honestly, I don't think so. Except share a little of your wonderful insight. I'm completely baffled by the whole thing right now."

"Sounds like you need some on-the-scene help. I'd be on the next flight, but I have a big paper due. I do want you to promise not to take any unnecessary chances, though."

"Come on, Ned, you know me. I'm always very careful," Nancy said, teasing him.

"Yes, I know. That's why I want you to keep a low profile. I want you to be in one piece the next time I see you."

Nancy blew a kiss into the phone and said goodbye. After she hung up, she smiled sadly. If only Ned were able to meet her in New York . . .

Just then, the front doorbell rang. Nancy went to open it, and before her stood Mattie Jensen. Her rich auburn hair was pulled up in a ponytail, and she was wearing jeans and a sweatshirt. She looked almost as young as Nancy.

"Hiya, kiddo!" the actress said, bubbling. "Eloise told me she was going to the ballet tonight, so I thought you guys might want a little company."

How could anyone as beautiful and successful as Mattie Jensen be all alone at ten o'clock on a Saturday night? Nancy wondered. It didn't seem possible. But there she was. She's lonely! Nancy realized.

"Sure. Come on in," she said. "Bess is in the shower."

"Hey, I read about what happened to you today on the boat trip. After everything he's been through, Rick must be glad they caught the guy. They said the man tried to throw him overboard."

"Hmm-hmm," Nancy replied, wishing she could have shared Mattie's sense of relief.

"They said the guy was released from a mental institution a few weeks ago."

"I didn't hear that, but from the way he was acting . . ." Nancy's voice trailed off.

"Oh, Nancy, I'm so relieved. Now I'll finally be able to sleep at night!" Mattie smiled softly, but Nancy just turned away. "What's the matter, Nancy? Are you still upset?"

Nancy heaved an enormous sigh. "Mattie, I hate to say this. I know you're not going to like it, but I don't think the man they arrested today is the person we're after."

"But—but they said he'd been stalking Rick for weeks."

"He may have been, but I don't think he's the one who tampered with the light, and sent the chocolates."

Mattie gazed at Nancy in amazement. Then she nodded. "Okay. Tell me why you think it isn't the same person."

"Two reasons. For starters, someone tried to run Rick over tonight."

"No!" Mattie exclaimed.

"I'm afraid so. Don't try to tell Rick that —he insists it was a hit-and-run accident. But I was there, Mattie. The cab never blew its horn, never slowed down—and the license plate was covered over with mud. This all may be circumstantial evidence, but still . . ."

Mattie was silent, taking it all in. "And then," Nancy said, continuing, "there's the photograph of Rick, the one that was all scratched up. It wasn't just a publicity shot, the kind he might autograph for a fan. There was a résumé of all the shows he's been in stapled to the back of it. Correct me if I'm wrong, but actors don't just give out their résumés to the general public, do they?"

"No, of course not. But lots of people would have them."

"Like who? A producer?"

"Sure. When an actor auditions for a job, he always brings a picture and résumé," she said, sitting down. "Pappas would have them. So would the director, and Lillian, of course. His agent would have hundreds. I suppose even Dwayne might have a few left, unless he cleaned out his files recently." Mattie stared at the wall with a faraway look. "But Dwayne is harmless. I'm sure—"

"Wait. Why Dwayne? I thought Rick said he was with International Management."

"Yes, but when Rick was first in New York, Dwayne was his agent. The summer I first met both of them, we were in an acting company doing Shakespeare in Oregon. We were so sure of ourselves," she mused. "Anyway, that fall, we set out for New York and the 'big time.' Rick and I did all right, but Dwayne, who was trying to make it as an actor still, ran into trouble getting parts. He was the wrong type somehow. So, he decided to open a talent agency instead. He really got our careers moving, too."

Just then Bess stepped into the room, a terry bathrobe wrapped around her. "I thought I heard somebody! Hi, Mattie," she chirped. "Did Nancy tell you about our day? Kind of wild, huh?"

"I read about part of it in the paper," Mattie said. "It was—" The telephone rang, interrupting her.

"That's probably for me!" Bess said as she dove for the phone. "Oh, hi!" she purred into the receiver. "Yes, I thought you might— Really? Hmmm—" Suddenly Bess turned a deep crimson and let out a wild giggle. "Umm, just a minute," she said. "I think I'll take this in the other room."

Carefully putting the receiver on its side, Bess gestured wildly at Nancy and then the phone. "It's Rick!" she whispered excitedly. "Hang up for me, okay?" With that, she ran into the bedroom.

Nancy turned to Mattie. She was pale and her glamorous face was drawn tight. Staring vacantly toward the bedroom, her enormous eyes began to fill with tears.

Nancy replaced the receiver. "Mattie . . ." she murmured gently, "you still love him, don't you?"

Mattie collapsed back into her chair. "Yes, I do. Heaven knows why," she answered. "Just a habit, I guess. I've loved him since I first saw him. We've been through a lot together."

Nancy put her hand comfortingly on Mattie's arm. As they listened to Bess giggling happily in the other room, Nancy could feel Mattie's grief. If a girl were talking with Ned like that, she'd be crushed, too.

"But then," Mattie said with a sad smile, "Rick obviously doesn't feel the same way. Well, I'd better go. I might as well get some sleep. We're still having brunch tomorrow morning, right?"

Nancy nodded and walked Mattie to the door, watching as she went down the stairs to her garden apartment. Just as the actress was about to disappear, Nancy remembered what she had been thinking before the phone rang.

"Mattie! Wait!" she called.

The actress looked up from the stairwell. "Yes?"

"How could I get into Dwayne Casper's office? I'd just like to take a look around."

"Well," said Mattie, her brow wrinkling as she thought, "I suppose you could set up an appointment and say you were an aspiring actress. You could even say we did a show together once."

"That might work. I don't think he ever noticed me before. Whenever I saw him I wasn't near you or him. But I don't have any pictures or résumés," she reminded Mattie.

"Oh, that's okay," Mattie assured her. "Just tell him you're new in town. Ask him for advice—he loves that. Dwayne's really good with newcomers, and he'll be flattered that you came to him for guidance. If you call first thing Monday morning and say I told you to call, I guarantee you'll get in. But I promise you, Dwayne is harmless. I should know—we've been friends for years."

"I hope you're right. But if Dwayne's got anything to do with this, I've got to find out. And, Mattie," she said softly, "don't worry about Bess. I know her. She falls in and out of love all the time. She'll get over Rick as soon as she gets back home, you'll see."

Mattie stared into the distance, trying to hide her feelings. "Maybe," she murmured softly. Giving Nancy a strange look, she disappeared down the stairwell to her apartment. Nancy could hear her door close behind her.

That night, tossing and turning in her bed, Nancy couldn't sleep. Her eyes kept popping open, and she'd lie still and stare at the ceiling while her mind was in high gear and she worked through detail after detail. If only they added up.

Rick Arlen. She could picture his handsome face with that winning grin of his, and those sparkling azure eyes. Someone wanted him dead, but who? Rick might not win any popularity contests among the people who knew him best, but only one person hated him enough to want him dead.

It took a very clever person to conceal such powerful hatred so successfully. Nancy tried to imagine who it might be, but there were so many people wishing him ill: Pappas, Casper, Lillian Weiss, and who knows how many others there were just on the set alone. Nancy had had cases this difficult before, and she'd solved them successfully. But this time there were so many possibilities; which one should she investigate first?

As she drifted to sleep, the shadowy figure of Rick came back into her mind. He was signing autographs for a crowd of fans. A monstrous figure walked toward him, slowly stalking him. Nancy tried to cry out, but her voice was caught in her throat. The figure turned toward her, seeing her for the first time. Eyes of indescribable evil glowed at her, paralyzing her with fear.

Then the figure drew a long and sharp knife that glinted in the dim light. Nancy tried to scream, but nothing happened. The shadowy figure was getting closer and closer—

Nancy awoke with a gasp and sat up in bed. The clock-radio by her bed read 5:05 A.M. It was only a dream, thank goodness! she thought, her heart racing. But it was so real.

Sighing with relief, she turned over, ready to

go back to sleep. That's when she noticed that Bess's bed was empty.

In an instant, Nancy was up and out of bed. She hurried into the kitchen—no Bess. She checked the bathroom, the living room, then ran back to the bedroom. Nothing. It couldn't be, but it was.

Bess was gone!

Chapter

Ten

THE SOUND OF a car pulling up in front of the building sent Nancy to the window. Opening it and leaning out, she saw a shiny black limousine gleaming in the light of a streetlamp.

A second later Bess stepped out onto the sidewalk. She was followed by Rick, who wrapped his arm around her shoulder. "You won't mind if I don't walk you to the door, will you?" hc asked, just loud enough for Nancy to hcar.

Bess twirled around and leaned closer into his arms. "Of course not," she said. "I had a great time. It was fun, zipping around the city, just the two of us. Thanks." They fell into a kiss that seemed as if it would never end.

Standing at the window, Nancy was alarmed. As flighty as Bess could be, it wasn't like her to sneak off in the middle of the night. Rick had gone to Bess's head like bubbly champagne. Nancy could only hope her friend wasn't in for a nasty "hangover" when it was all over.

"Nancy!" Bess called out in surprise when she saw her friend waiting for her at the door to the apartment. "What are you doing up?"

"Excuse me," Nancy answered in a low voice, careful not to wake her aunt. "But what are *you* doing up is the question."

Bess's eyes were sparkling. "Oh, Nancy," she said breathily. "New York is so *wonderful!* I've never really noticed before how incredible it is. I just have to live here someday. *Soon.*" Turning to her friend, Bess continued, "We went everywhere. We rode around Wall Street and went to the South Street Seaport and then to this incredible disco, Le Grandine. Absolutely everyone there knew Rick. And he likes me. I mean, he really likes *me!* This could be it! This could be the man I've been looking for all my life!"

"Bess," Nancy began as gently as she could, "didn't you think it might be just a little dangerous to be going out with Rick in the middle of the night when someone is trying to kill him?"

Bess looked annoyed. "Don't spoil this for me, okay?" She walked past Nancy into the apartment and went to their room.

Nancy glared at her friend as she disappeared down the hall. Bess could be so irritating sometimes. Earlier that day she had narrowly missed getting herself killed, and here she was laughing in the face of danger. "You think I'm being silly?" Nancy asked, following after her.

"Of course I do! They arrested the guy, didn't they? Rick convinced me that the runaway cab was only an accident. Besides, nobody would mess with Rick. You should feel his muscles—they're like steel!"

Bess slipped out of her satiny dress and kicked off the slingbacks she had worn to go dancing. Too tired to change into a nightgown, she fell back on the bed in her lacy pink slip.

"Oh, Nancy," she murmured excitedly. "He's so wonderful—and so cute." Reaching over, she snapped off the light between their beds. "Am I going to have happy dreams tonight!"

As Nancy lay in her bed, watching the light of dawn brighten the room, she couldn't help worrying about Bess. This was obviously more than just a schoolgirl crush. And Nancy was more convinced than ever that this fairy-tale romance was not going to have a happy ending.

The clock by Nancy's bed read 9:04 A.M. Bess was still asleep, a contented smile on her lips. Nancy figured she'd be out for a few more hours.

The apartment was quiet. Looking out the window, Nancy saw only one person on the street. The whole city seemed to still be asleep. At eleven, she'd be going out to brunch with her aunt and Mattie, but that was still two hours away.

After pulling on her favorite jeans and slipping her new yellow sweater over her head, Nancy decided that a walk might be just what she needed to help her think and unwind.

Stepping out onto the street, Nancy took a deep breath of the fresh spring air. The birds were singing, and the golden-green leaves on the trees swayed in the morning breeze. On this quiet Sunday morning, with church bells ringing in the distance, New York seemed like a small nineteenth-century town. Nancy loved it. As she walked, she imagined she was part of that older, simpler time.

After a while she came to a tiny park tucked between two buildings. The morning sun was just beginning to warm the benches, and a few people were out with their children, pushing them on swings and watching as they ran and played. Nancy couldn't help herself; she sat down on a bench and let the sun warm her face, relaxing for the first time in days.

A minute later the touch of a hand on her shoulder made Nancy jump. Glancing around, she found herself looking into the dark eyes of Lillian Weiss.

"Well, if it isn't our fair rescuer," Lillian smirked. "Fancy meeting you here."

Nancy was puzzled. New York was a huge city. The odds of running into someone that she knew were small, to say the least.

"Mind if I sit down?" Lillian asked casually. "I'm dead tired. Haven't slept all night."

Nancy moved over to make room for her. She felt uncomfortable in the company of such an unpleasant person, but she didn't want to be impolite.

"Are you still trying to save Rick Arlen's life?" Lillian asked suddenly, looking right into Nancy's eyes.

She certainly is blunt, Nancy thought. Well, I might as well be blunt right back. Whoever was trying to kill Rick already knew that she was on the case. "Still trying," she admitted.

"You really shouldn't bother," Lillian said. She looked down at her feet, so Nancy couldn't read her expression.

"I don't understand," said Nancy, prompting her.

Lillian looked at her curiously, as if she were sizing Nancy up. After what seemed an eternity, she fixed her eyes on Nancy. "Rick is going to die, and there's nothing you can do about it. And I'll tell you something else—whatever happens to him, he has coming. He got where he is by stepping on a lot of people, but he made one mistake. Along the way he stepped on the *wrong* person, and he's going to pay for it."

Nancy couldn't believe what she was hearing. Was this a confession? A warning? She wasn't sure how to take Lillian's statement.

As suddenly as she had appeared, Lillian stood up to leave. "Well," she said, fingering the hem of her purple lamb's-wool sweater, "nice running into you." She gazed at Nancy with a tight smile. "I'll say one thing for you—you've got guts."

Nancy watched as the strange young woman walked away. She was sure now that Lillian had deliberately arranged to run into her. But why? Nancy was more in the dark than ever.

"The restaurant we're going to isn't far away, Nancy. We'll just ring for Mattie on our way out." Eloise was standing in front of the hall mirror, fussing with a teal blue silk scarf. "Is Bess ready yet?"

"Bess!" Nancy called as she knocked on the

door of the room where her friend lay sleeping. "Don't you want to have brunch with us?"

The answer was muffled, so Nancy opened the door. "Leave the address," was all Bess could manage. "I'll meet you there." With that, she flopped over and buried her face in the pillow.

Nancy closed the door. Eloise waited by the main door of the apartment while Nancy wrote down the address and left it on the telephone table. "Ah, youth," Eloise said, smiling wistfully. "I used to be able to sleep like that on weekend mornings. Now I'm always up at the crack of dawn!"

With a wink, Eloise tugged on Nancy's arm. "Shall we? If I wait for my morning coffee much longer, I won't be worth knowing."

As they sat in the restaurant eating eggs Benedict, Nancy couldn't stop thinking of her conversation with Lillian Weiss. The look in her eyes had been so intense. Could it be that Lillian was the one who was trying to kill Rick? Or maybe she was just hiding the identity of the person who really was.

Nancy decided not to mention running into her. Still, she had to know what Lillian's personal situation regarding Rick was. "Mattie," she began offhandedly, "tell me more about Lillian Weiss. I know you said lots

93

of people hate Rick, but she seems to hate him more than most."

Mattie looked up, amazed. "You don't think she's behind it all, do you?"

"I don't really know," Nancy replied. "But I'd like to know more about her."

"Lillian's the one Rick broke up with me for," Mattie blurted out. She looked down at her plate unhappily. "I couldn't believe it when he told me. I mean, I'd stuck by him through all the bad times. When he finally made it, he just dropped me. It was so—" she paused for a moment, unable to go on "—so humiliating." She took out her handkerchief and blew her nose. Suddenly Mattie laughed. "But that's Rick for you. They were only together for two months. He stuck with her till she introduced him to the film people she knew, then he dumped her. I really can't blame Lillian for hating him. I just wish she'd get on with her life. She's just—I don't know —the kind of person who nurses a grudge. The kind that never lets go of anything, know what I mean?"

"Yes," said Nancy thoughtfully. "I think I do."

"Oh, do I dare try one of these?" Eloise was asking with a smile as the waiter held up a plate of miniature pastries.

"Oh, go ahead, Eloise," Mattie said with a

grin, trying to put all thoughts of Rick and Lillian behind her.

Eloise looked at the pastries and thought for a moment. "Why not?" she quipped, lifting a small one onto her plate.

Just then, the manager came up to the table. "Excuse me, ladies. Is there a Nancy Drew at this table?"

"Why, yes," Eloise answered, looking at her niece.

"Ms. Drew, you have a phone call," the manager said. "You can pick it up at the main desk by the coatrack."

"It must be Bess," Eloise guessed. "She probably woke up and realized she'd never be able to make it here after all."

Nancy thanked the manager and made her way to the phone.

"Hi, Bess," she said into the receiver.

But it wasn't Bess. A raspy electronic voice warned her, "Stay away from Rick Arlen, Nancy Drew! And tell your little friend she'd better stay away, too!" With that, the phone line went dead in Nancy's trembling hand.

Chapter

Eleven

By Appointment Only!" "Put Your Picture And Résumé Under The Door!" "Do Not Ring Buzzer Without An Appointment!"

Nancy read the signs and gulped. Although she'd called earlier and left a message on Dwayne's answering machine, Nancy felt she'd have a better chance of seeing him if she went in person. But getting inside Dwayne Casper's office wasn't exactly going to be easy.

With a sigh and a deep breath, she pressed the buzzer. For a moment it was so quiet that she wondered whether anybody was in the office at all. Then, crisp footsteps sounded on the other side of the door.

"Do you have an appointment?" Dwayne's voice was all business.

"Well, no," Nancy replied. "Not exactly."

"In that case, I suggest you learn to read!"

"But, Mr. Casper!" Nancy said in her most polite voice. "I left a message on your machine. Mattie Jensen said you would talk to me. My name is Diane Elliot. . . ."

Nancy heard a click as he unlocked the door. It swung open, and a smiling Dwayne Casper greeted her. "Well, why didn't you just say you're a friend of Mattie's?" he asked. "Come in! You must understand that if I opened the door to every struggling actor in this town, I'd never be able to get any work done."

"Oh, thank you, Mr. Casper," Nancy said, sounding grateful. In the front reception area was a large empty desk. No receptionist, Nancy noted.

"Right this way," Dwayne said with a sugary smile. He led her into his plush office. "How do you know Mattie?"

"Oh, well, I was an extra on 'Danner's Dream,' and she was kind enough to talk to me. She did say she'd call you about me. But I guess she got busy." That much was true, Nancy thought.

Dwayne settled into his chair and looked at her appraisingly. "So you know Luther Parks too?"

"Well, no. Not personally, that is."

"I see. Has Mattie ever seen your work? Apart from extra work, that is."

Here we go, Nancy thought. Time to start lying—and lying big. "Oh, yes," she assured him. "We did a production of *The Sound of Music* together in the Midwest. Mattie played the oldest daughter, and I played one of the younger children."

An amused look passed over Dwayne's face. "That must have been at least eight years ago. Mattie wasn't more than a kid herself back then. Unfortunately, I couldn't see that production."

I know, Nancy thought. That's what Mattie told me.

Dwayne leaned back in his swivel chair. He seemed warm now, even friendly. "So, let me guess, you've come to the big city because you want to be a real actress."

Delighted that the agent had bought her story, Nancy threw herself into her real-life acting role. "Yes, sir," she answered breathlessly.

"Well, well, well— What shall we do about that?" Dwayne pursed his lips, thinking. Then he stood up, walked to the door, and locked it. "So we won't be disturbed," he explained.

A sudden chill made its way down Nancy's spine. If the electronic voice on the phone yesterday had been Dwayne's, she was now trapped.

"What did you say your name was?" Dwayne had a pen poised over a small pink index card.

"Diane Elliot," Nancy said, looking the agent squarely in the eye. "With two *L*s and one *T.*"

"That's a good name for an actress. You're lucky." He smiled. "Now tell me, Diane, why did you come to me? There are hundreds of agents in this city."

"Well, Mattie spoke so highly of you, Mr. Casper," Nancy began. Dwayne's face grew pink with pleasure. "And I know you once represented Rick Arlen—"

At the mention of Rick's name, the agent's face clouded over. "Ah, yes, the irrepressible Mr. A."

"He's not with you anymore, is he?" Nancy was being bolder than she liked to be, but she had to lead Dwayne on.

"Rick? His real name is Richard Aburtuski, by the way. No, he's no longer one of my clients. I don't deal with failures, Ms. Elliot."

Nancy looked genuinely surprised. Dwayne laughed derisively. "You think I'm being ridiculous—after all, he's at the height of success! But I can tell you with certainty that leaving this agency is the biggest mistake Arlen ever made—except for his decision to be an actor, of course. The man can't act his way out of a paper bag. He depends on his looks to get him by, but he'll learn. They all learn eventually that the biggest factor in success is loyalty. And he has none."

Dwayne's face was red with anger. He wasn't through on the subject of Rick Arlen, but just then the buzzer rang. "Whoever it is will go away," he said. "I have no appointments scheduled today."

The buzzer rang through the office once again, and then again and again. Finally Dwayne couldn't stand it anymore. He bolted from his chair and unlocked the door. "I'm going to tell this idiot to go away. Do you have an appointment?" he yelled, hurrying through the reception area. "Because if you don't, you'd better learn to read!"

"But, Mr. Casper! You *must* see me!" Bess's voice was muffled through the door, but her sense of urgency came through loud and clear. "I'm a really great actress and I need an agent! Let me read for you, Mr. Casper, and you can judge for yourself!"

Laughing bitterly, Dwayne called through the door. "Young lady, I'm a very busy man, and I don't handle street performers. Please leave me alone."

"But I'm an *actress!* Just listen." Bess began to recite a passage from *Romeo and Juliet.*

Good old Bess, Nancy thought with a smile. She really was quite an actress when she had to be. They had devised a plan: After Nancy was able to get inside Dwayne's office, Bess would divert his attention so that Nancy could search it. As soon as Dwayne was out of sight in the reception area, Nancy began to rummage through the papers on his desk. The longer Bess was able to divert his attention from Nancy, the more Nancy would be able to find out. And from the sound of things, Nancy thought she just might have all day.

"And I sing, too! Just listen to this, Mr. Casper." Bess launched into a well-known show tune in a loud, off-key voice.

"Please, young woman!" Dwayne begged. "Why don't you go sing in the park or something? You're giving me a headache!"

Aha! Nancy's eyes opened wide as she looked at the papers in front of her. An eviction notice—and several large bills from creditors. Searching further, she found warnings from collection agencies, even threats. Dwayne Casper's talent agency was obviously in desperate trouble.

"But, Mr. Casper, I'm the next Mattie Jensen! Everyone says I look just like her, except I'm prettier."

"What?" Dwayne exploded. *"Nobody,* but *nobody,* ever was, is, or will be prettier than Mattie Jensen! Mattie is one of a kind —absolutely unique!"

101

Nancy cocked her head to listen. It was clear to her that, where Mattie was concerned, Dwayne's interest was more than just professional.

"Well, I'm unique, too, Mr. Casper—terribly unique and incredibly talented!"

"My dear young woman"—Dwayne was practically screaming now—"if you don't leave at once, I'll call the police. And may I say in parting that with your nerve, you'll probably go far in this business!"

Quickly Nancy put everything back in the desk exactly where she'd found it. When Dwayne returned, he was trying hard to calm down.

"I'm sorry. Now, where were we before that ghastly woman interrupted us?"

Nancy shifted uncomfortably in her seat. Dwayne's eyes had a wild look in them, and having found what she'd come for, all she wanted to do was get out as quickly as she could.

"You know, Mr. Casper, I feel like such a fool, but I just remembered—I've got an appointment with a photographer in fifteen minutes! He's going to take head shots of me."

"Oh, I see," Dwayne replied, still smiling. "Well, is he any good? Maybe I know him. What's his name?"

"His name? Uh—" Nancy panicked for a

moment. What could she say? Finally she blurted out, "Ned Nickerson. He's new in town—just got in from L.A. But Mattie says he's good."

"Hmmm." Dwayne frowned. "Never heard of him. Well, Diane, come and see me when you've got your pictures. I'll see what I can do for you." He extended his hand for her to shake. His grip was firm, like iron, and his eyes searched hers intently.

"Come to think of it, have we met before? You look a bit familiar," Dwayne said.

"Well, we've never actually met," she replied, "but as I said before, I did do extra work on 'Danner's Dream'."

"That must be it, then," he said. "You'd better get going if you don't want to be late for your shoot. Look forward to seeing you again, Ms. Elliot."

"Thank you so much. You've been a great help!" Nancy said and left the office.

Down in the lobby, Bess was munching on a candy bar and smiling broadly. "How'd I do?" she mumbled, her mouth full of chocolate.

"Bravo!" Nancy applauded, laughing. "I especially loved your rendition of 'Tonight.' It was—different, very different."

"You really think so?" asked Bess, fluffing her hair and winking.

"And wait till I tell you what I found!" Nancy said, grabbing her friend by the arm. "But we'd better get over to 'Danner's Dream' right away. I want Mattie to hear this, too."

The crisp spring air whirled around them as they walked briskly up Broadway toward Columbus Avenue.

"He's really in bad shape, huh?" Bess asked incredulously after Nancy filled her in.

"Everybody in the world is after him. And when people are that desperate, it can make them pretty crazy. I want to keep a close eye on Dwayne Casper, Bess. I think he may be our man."

Pushing through the glass doors of Worldwide Broadcasting, Nancy and Bess beamed at the security guard.

"Hi!" Nancy called out. "We're back again."

"Why, hello, girls. You heard the set was closed, didn't you?" the man asked. "They've been having a little trouble in there and Pappas sent down the order. I can't let anybody in, not even you two."

"I know," Nancy told him. "But could you call Mattie Jensen? We just need to talk to her for a few minutes."

The security guard ran his finger down the list of telephone extensions on his desk. "Sure thing. Mattie, let's see— Ah! Here it is."

But before he had a chance to pick up the

intercom, he was interrupted by the boom of a powerful explosion. The sound of shattering glass tore through the air, followed by a blood-curdling scream.

"Nancy!" gasped Bess in terror. "That was Rick!"

Chapter

Twelve

Without waiting for permission, Nancy and Bess followed the security guard backstage. Losing themselves in a mob of people, the girls made their way toward Rick's dressing room.

The lighting designer had been the first to reach the room itself. "Call an ambulance!" he bellowed frantically.

Nancy and Bess arrived a minute later and watched in shock as Kay Wills, the makeup artist, staggered down the hall toward them. Her skin was ashen, and she was trembling all over. Choking back tears, she turned around and sobbed, "It's bad—really bad."

Nancy stood on tiptoe and craned her neck to see inside Rick's dressing room. The first thing that caught her eye was the wide mirror over the makeup table. It had been shattered into a thousand pieces!

An emergency medical team had arrived, and they were on their way up the hall now, pushing aside the crowd of onlookers. "Make room!" Nancy called, flattening herself against the wall.

"Rick! Oh, where is he?" Bess cried frantically. She bit the back of her hand as she strained to get a good look. Just then, Rick appeared in the doorway. He had a stunned look on his face. His blond hair had been blown every which way, and the white towel around his shoulders was stained bright red. Looking down, Nancy gasped—Rick's hands were bleeding!

As soon as the paramedics saw him, they broke into a run. Gathering around him, they picked him up and laid him on a stretcher. They began pulling slivers of glass out of his hands as Rick winced in pain.

"Back off, everybody!" one of the paramedics shouted as the crowd began to press in on them again. In what seemed like just a few seconds, they had finished their immediate task and lifted the stretcher. They carried the wounded star down the hall, out of the building, and into a waiting ambulance.

Once Rick was gone, the bystanders milled around, not knowing what to do. The police arrived and began inspecting the scene, interviewing people, and collecting evidence.

Nancy walked over to Kay, who was now sitting on the floor in a corner of the hall. She still looked pale as a ghost.

"What happened, Kay?" Nancy asked gently, crouching down beside her.

"He was w-wiping off h-his cold cream—" Kay stammered, staring off into space. "And the mirror just exploded! Thank God he had that towel over his face. He'd be blind —worse, maybe. And I was just on my way in there—it could have been me, too!"

A few minutes later, while police combed the area for clues, Pappas assembled the cast and crew.

"Listen up! I have a report from the hospital about Rick." The excited buzzing died down as the producer's voice boomed out into the vast studio.

"He's going to be okay. They said it looked a lot worse than it really was, and that they're going to release him tonight. His hands will be bandaged for a while, of course, but we can work around that. I've already contacted our writers to come up with some material that'll explain his bandaged hands. If we can't work this into the story line somehow, Luther will just stick to closeups. In any case, we're not going to let this shut us down. As far as I'm concerned, you're all still under contract, and that includes Rick. I want everybody back here tomorrow at seven sharp!"

Just then the police officer who had been examining Rick's dressing room let out a long low whistle. "Hey, chief! Look what we found!"

The policeman held up a small metal object. "It's a twenty-four-hour timer. Whoever set this up must have done it yesterday."

Pappas, standing a few feet away, nearly choked. "That's impossible! This set is closed down tight on Sunday. I even hired extra security. My own mother couldn't have gotten in here!"

"Which means," said the chief, "that it was probably an inside job."

Now Nancy finally had a definite lead. She could rule out Dwayne Casper. He couldn't have gotten onto the set to plant the bomb.

But that left her with only two other suspects—Pappas and Lillian. Their faces floated in front of her tightly shut eyes as she leaned against the wall, trying to concentrate amid the confusion.

Nancy shook her head and opened her eyes. She was back at square one with a dangerous killer still on the loose right under her nose!

I've got to get out of here, she suddenly realized.

Quickly, Nancy sprang up and elbowed her way through a group of technicians hovering by the studio door. "Come on," she shouted to Bess. "We've got to go!"

Pulling her friend by the arm, Nancy made straight for the front exit. But she stopped short when she saw Lillian standing directly in front of her, a smug smile on her face. "I'm way ahead of you, Miss Teen Detective," she said, smirking. "Way ahead."

"What's wrong with her?" Bess wanted to know as they hailed a taxi on the corner. "She gives me the creeps."

Nancy didn't answer. She told the cab driver the name of the hospital as they piled in. "And hurry," she added.

Stepping off the elevator on the fifth floor, Nancy and Bess had no trouble finding Rick's room. It was the one with the two police officers in front of it.

Oh, well, thought Nancy, at least he's safe in there. Still, she couldn't help feeling as though she had failed miserably. The police were in on the case now, so there wasn't much point in continuing her investigation. And besides, she hadn't managed to come up with very much, had she?

"Sorry, miss. You can't go in this room,"

one of the officers told Bess when she tried to enter.

"I must see Rick," Bess said frantically.

"A Miss Jensen's in there with Mr. Arlen now."

Bess froze. "Oh. I see—" she finally managed to say. "Has she been there very long?"

"Ever since we got here, miss. About half an hour." He cracked open the door to look inside. "Seems like she might be awhile longer, too."

Bess stepped back, staring anxiously at the half-open door. Through it, she could hear Rick's voice. And it was not the voice of a confident TV star.

"Mattie! Oh, Mattie, I'm so scared. Someone really is trying to kill me!"

"Don't worry, my darling," she replied in a soft voice. "The police are here. They'll protect you."

"You know, Mattie, you were right all along. You were the only one who saw the truth. Mattie, if I come out of this mess alive, I swear I'm going to make everything up to you. I need you, Mattie, I need you so badly—no one else ever meant a thing to me. You're the only one I've ever loved!"

"I've heard enough!" Bess turned and ran down the hall, covering her mouth with her hands.

"Bess! Bess, wait!" Nancy called after her.

"Leave me alone!" She was fighting back her tears but losing the battle. "I can't believe it," she sobbed. "I just can't believe it!"

Nancy started to go after Bess but thought better of it. Right then Bess needed to work this out on her own. But Nancy wondered about the force of her friend's reaction. What was it about this guy that caused women to fall instantly in love with him?

Mattie and Rick had stopped talking, and the police officer silently closed the door again. No sense waiting around, Nancy decided.

Out on the sidewalk, Nancy found Bess. Her eyes were brimming over with tears, and her mascara was smeared all over her face. She looked utterly forlorn.

"Come on, Bess. Let's go home," Nancy suggested, gently taking her friend's hand. Bess nodded listlessly, allowing herself to be led.

The two friends were silent all the way back to Eloise's apartment. Looking over at Bess, Nancy wished she could comfort her somehow. She knew that Bess really hurt. Bess's brave hero had turned out to be not so brave after all. And worse than that, he was in love with someone else.

As they got out of the cab, Nancy caught sight of her aunt Eloise entering the building. "Hi, Aunt Eloise," she called as she hurried up to greet her.

"Hi, Nancy—Bess," she said as they entered the building. "Did you have a nice day?"

"You're never going to believe what happened today," Bess said in a soft voice. She had finally gotten control of herself.

"Well, as soon as we get upstairs, let's kick off our shoes and relax, and you can tell me all about it," Eloise replied, moving toward the mailboxes.

The three were in the mail alcove when Eloise looked down and spotted a small box wrapped in brown paper on the package table. She glanced at it and scooped it up. "Nancy, it's addressed to you," she said, noticing it had no stamps.

As she started to hand it to Nancy, she froze. The box was ticking!

Chapter

Thirteen

Nancy SPRANG INTO action. "Bess, get on the house phone and get someone to call the police."

While Bess was contacting a neighbor, Nancy and Eloise examined the package. "I think the ticking sounds different now," Nancy's aunt said in a frightened whisper. She was still holding the box, but now in trembling hands. "Let's take it outside."

Slowly and calmly, the two went out of the building and walked to the curb. As soon as they had stopped and put the box down, two police bomb-squad officers arrived. It didn't take them long to discover that the box contained an ordinary, harmless alarm clock.

"I've never been so happy to see an alarm clock in my entire life." Nancy's aunt smiled with relief and clasped her hands together to stop them from shaking.

"Somebody went to a lot of trouble to scare your niece, ma'am. And from the sound of this note, that person is serious."

"'Last warning, Nancy Drew, leave town *now*,'" the officer read.

"Nancy, I think maybe we *should* get back to River Heights today." Bess had rejoined them and stood listening as the note was read.

"Bess is right, Nancy. This is serious. Your father would never forgive me if anything happened to you while you were here. Worse, I would never forgive myself. In fact, after the officers leave, I'm calling the airport."

Eloise, Nancy, and Bess thanked the men, and they turned and headed back into the building and up to Eloise's apartment.

Nancy bit her lip. "Wait a minute, Aunt Eloise," she said, trying to stop her aunt from calling the airport. She knew her aunt was only trying to protect her, but how could she leave New York while a dangerous killer was still after Rick? Even if he wasn't the greatest guy in the world, he didn't deserve to die. And obviously, the killer was getting closer and closer. Next time he might succeed.

"Our tickets are for the day after tomorrow," she called out as her aunt was about to lift the phone. "Maybe I can solve the case before then."

"Forget it, Nancy. I'm not going to let you risk your life—not even for a couple more days." Eloise sounded definite. "And besides, the police are on the case now."

"She's probably right, Nancy," Bess agreed.

"Wait a minute, everybody." Nancy was groping for the right words. "You can't ask me to just walk away from this! A man's life is in danger!"

They looked back at her with questioning stares, unconvinced.

"How about this—I promise that if I don't come up with any answers by tomorrow, I'll go straight back to River Heights as we planned originally. But honestly, I could never live with myself if I knew I'd walked away when I could have helped."

Eloise looked down at the floor. Nancy had gotten to her. Bess, despite everything, had to smile. Sleuthing was in Nancy's blood.

"All right, Nancy," Eloise said reluctantly. "I do have only myself to blame—I did introduce you to Mattie."

"Thanks, Aunt Eloise," Nancy cried warmly, throwing her arms around the older woman's shoulders. "You're a peach, you know that?"

"Some peach. I invite you to New York for a vacation, and you wind up running all over town, tracking down a murderer. And getting bomb threats delivered to your door!"

"He or she is *not* a murderer—not yet, anyway," Nancy said. "Nobody's been killed, and I hope we can keep it that way. Now, if you'll excuse me, there's something I've got to take care of right away."

"Who's there?" came Mattie's surprised voice in response to Nancy's knock.

"It's me. May I come in?"

"Oh, Nancy," Mattie said when she opened the door. "Wasn't it awful?" Mattie looked exhausted. Obviously, she had just been through quite an ordeal. "Come on in," she added distractedly. "Sorry the place is such a mess. I just got back from the hospital."

"How's Rick doing?" Nancy asked.

"He's going to be okay. But—oh, Nancy, his hands! They hurt him terribly. I just can't believe he's actually going to do the show tomorrow."

"What?" she gasped. "Tomorrow?"

Nancy was truly amazed—he had sounded so frightened at the hospital. I have to give him a lot of credit, she thought. He really was brave.

"Pappas showed up at the hospital. He just burst in past the guards. I was there for the whole thing. He couldn't stop apologizing for this and all the other things that have been happening on the set lately. He even promised to hire Rick a bodyguard and to get some plainclothes detectives to be at the studio until this whole thing is over. But Rick said something about loyalty to his fellow actors, and just shrugged it off and told Pappas he'd be back at work tomorrow. As shaken up as Rick was, he just couldn't say no." She sighed miserably.

"I don't know how I'm going to get through tomorrow," she said. "I'm so worried about him. Oh, Nancy, what am I going to do? If he's killed, I'll just—I'll—oh, I don't know what I'll do!" Mattie seemed to be on the brink of hysteria.

"Hold on, Mattie. It's going to be okay," said Nancy, trying to comfort her. "I'm still here, and I've got one more day in town. I haven't given up yet."

Mattie looked into Nancy's eyes, and a glimmer of hope showed on her face. "You —you mean it?"

"Mmm-hmm. Maybe I'm not exactly closer to solving this case, but I sure know a lot more than when I started. And I'll do my best for you until it's time for me to leave," Nancy assured her. "Please don't worry."

But what Nancy didn't tell Mattie was that

she was hoping the criminal would try again and this time make a mistake—the kind of mistake he or she had managed to avoid until then. Her experience showed that most criminals tripped themselves up sooner or later.

"Oh, I hope you're right," Mattie said with a nervous laugh. "I guess I'd better get you and Bess hired on as extras again, huh?"

When it was all arranged, Mattie went back to the hospital to get Rick, and Nancy went back upstairs for a quiet dinner with her aunt and Bess.

Just before turning in, she went into the empty living room, picked up the phone, and dialed. She was in luck.

"Twice in one week?" came Ned's familiar voice. "What's going on, Nancy? Could this be true love?"

Nancy giggled, with a wave of warm feeling passing over her. Good old Ned. He was just what she needed right then—the voice of sanity. "You know I love you," she said with a laugh. "But thanks for trying to be funny. I can use a little humor right now."

"Things aren't going too well there, are they?"

"That's putting it mildly," she said, and told him the latest developments in the case.

Ned tried to sound comforting. "Look, Nancy, I've known you for a long time, right?"

"Forever," she replied.

"And in all that time, I've never seen you blow a case. So just hang in there. You'll figure it out."

"But, Ned, I have only one more day!" she protested.

"Something will happen, and the pieces will all fall into place. You'll solve this one, I know you will, Detective Drew."

"Well, I'm glad somebody thinks so." She sighed, not really convinced. "I appreciate the vote of confidence, though."

"And, Nancy . . ."

"Yes, Ned?"

"Be careful, okay? I'd hate to have anything happen to you."

Once again, the girls were slated to play nurses. Rick's injuries had been written into the script. In the *new* story line, Rory, in a fit of despair, would try to throw himself out a window. He would be rescued, but not before he had cut his hands to pieces and had to be taken to the hospital.

"Nancy! How do I look?" Bess asked later that day. Twirling around in her nurse's uniform, she fluffed her red wig carefully so the pert white nurse's cap wouldn't fall off. Her heart didn't seem half as badly broken since she had found out she'd be working on "Danner's Dream" again that day. She even had a "silent bit"—she was the nurse who would greet Serena when she arrived at the hospital.

"I called my mother to make sure she'd tape the program," Bess said excitedly. "Then I can take it around to casting directors and stuff."

Nancy smiled at her friend. Even in the middle of all this craziness, she was still managing to have a good time. Of course, her fun was tempered by her feelings for Rick. Whenever she saw him on the set, she turned and purposely avoided him.

"Oh, and you know what? I found out that that lady with glasses and clipboard over there is the casting director," Bess whispered, pulling Nancy by the arm. "I'm going to go hang around her for a while. You never can tell, Nancy, this could be *it*. And won't Rick feel like a fool when I become a bigger star than he ever was!"

Nancy sighed and looked at her friend. "Bess, as a friend, I've got to tell you this: You are totally insane!" Then pushing her friend playfully, she whispered, "But go for it. I hope she notices you. I'll see you when it's time for our scene, okay? I want to check out Rick's new dressing room."

121

Rick was dressing and being made up in an improvised area across the hall from the costume room. He sat staring listlessly into space, still stunned by what had happened the day before. Kay was with him.

"So, Rick," she was saying, trying to cheer him up, "are you going to give me a hand here, or do I have to do this all myself?"

But Rick didn't move. He seemed so scared —as though there was a voice inside his head telling him over and over again that someone was trying to kill him. And that he or she might very well succeed.

Nancy leaned up against a wall and watched as Kay put some warm water into the sink. "No mirrors in here, I hope you've noticed," she said, trying to make a joke. When she saw she wasn't getting through to Rick even a little bit, she sighed wearily and picked up a stick of makeup.

"Okay, here we go," she said, uncapping it. Then, "Oops!" she cried as the stick slipped out of her hands and fell into the wet sink.

"Clumsy me," she said to herself, shaking her head. Suddenly, there was a hissing noise. The water in the sink began bubbling furiously.

"What the—?" Rick gasped. A sharp odor rose from the sink.

Nancy recognized the smell. "That's acid," she whispered.

"Oh, my God!" Kay cried, her hands on her cheeks as she watched the acid eat holes in the stainless steel sink. "Rick, that could have been your face!"

Chapter
Fourteen

"THAT'S IT!" RICK exclaimed, "I've had it!" He tried to pick up his suede jacket, but even a simple action such as this was difficult because of the bandages on his hands. Growling with disgust, he stormed out of the room.

"Rick?" Kay called, following him down the corridor. "Where are you going?"

"Forget it, Kay. I'm taking a nice long walk and going someplace where nobody can find me."

Just at that moment, a beet-faced William Pappas stepped into the hallway. "What's going on here?" he asked as the handsome actor flew down the hall.

"I'm out of here. Off the show. I'm not taking any more chances."

"But you're under contract, Arlen! You can't just leave!"

"Oh, yeah? Watch me." With that, Rick pushed past the angry producer and made his way toward the entrance.

Pappas made a lunge for him, but a couple of crew members restrained him.

"Come on, Mr. Pappas, calm down," they urged him. "Give him a break. The guy's been under a lot of stress lately."

Pappas let the men straighten his suit as he muttered under his breath, "He's under tension? What am I—chopped liver? I'm behind schedule, and the network is breathing down my back. I have ratings to think of!"

But it was too late. Rick was out the door and gone. Nancy and Kay looked on as the producer fumed, powerless to stop him.

Seconds later Luther Parks hurried up to them, running a hand nervously through his silver hair. "Bill, someone just said Rick Arlen left! What do you want me to do?"

But Pappas was in no mood for creative solutions. "You're the director," he snarled, heading back to his office. "Think of something!"

Luther shrugged and turned to Lillian, who was standing beside him. "We'll shoot the hospital scene with Mattie," he said.

"Whatever you say," Lillian drawled, throwing a wink Nancy's way. "Report to duty, Nurse Drew. And try not to miss your cue."

Standing in the make-believe operating room as the crew adjusted the lights, Nancy's spirits sank. Rick was out on the street somewhere, unprotected. And there she was on her last day in town, about to walk around in the background of a fictional scene instead of tracking down a very real criminal.

Someone had found a way to get around the set undetected, again and again. That was the key. In spite of guards at the doors, and people everywhere, Rick's enemy had gotten in. If she only knew how! If she could only discover the method behind the madness, she felt sure the rest would fall into place. But how could she do anything now?

"Action!" came Lillian's voice. Taking her medicine tray, Nancy crossed the set, put the tray down, and walked back again, heaving a deep sigh.

Action. That's exactly what was needed. If only there was some action she could take!

"Cheer up, Nancy." Bess peered sympathetically into the mirror at her friend's reflection. Nancy wasn't used to losing and it hurt. Bess pulled a comb through her blond hair and twisted it up in one deft move. She fastened it in place, and searched for something comforting to say. "I know it's a bummer, but you win some and you lose some." Somehow those weren't the words she had been looking for.

"Well, I don't really feel like going out to dinner, that's for sure," Nancy replied listlessly. She reached for her makeup case on the bathroom counter.

"But we're going to a really great restaurant! Your aunt, Eloise, said it's one of her favorites. And I can't wait to tell her about my big scene today. The videotape editor told me he was sure I got into the shot. Can you imagine? There I am, actually handing a paper to Mattie Jensen on national TV! My mother will flip!"

Nancy lifted the collar of her mauve jacket and fastened a rhinestone pin to the lapel. "There's just so little time left and so many unanswered questions."

Suddenly the door buzzer rang. "Come on, Nancy. That's the signal. Your aunt and the cab are waiting!" Bess cried. "Be right down!" she called into the intercom.

At the restaurant the girls were seated by a lovely young hostess, who looked more like a model than a restaurant employee.

"Pierre will be your waiter," she told them.

Just then, a young man with twinkling eyes and a handlebar mustache approached the table.

"Bonsoir. Je m'appelle Pierre. Here I haf ze menu," he said in a thick French accent. Bess couldn't help giggling as he handed the menus around the table, giving each of them a seductive look. "I can tell zees table will be my favorite of ze night."

"I didn't know this place served French food," Eloise mused out loud, watching him go.

"It doesn't," Bess remarked in surprise as she looked over the menu. "A French waiter at an American restaurant. That's weird."

"Not for New York it's not," Nancy's aunt replied.

Nancy's eyes followed the waiter to the bar, where he put in an order for some other customers. "Hey, Steve," he yelled in a regular voice, "give me three mineral waters and a Coke."

Nancy looked up when the waiter returned to the table to take their order. *"Garçon—avez vous un stylo noir, peut-être?"*

"Huh?" he asked, confused. "Want to run that by me again, lady?"

"You're *not* French?" Bess exclaimed.

"Mais non, mademoiselle," the waiter admitted with a shy smile. "I mean, nope. Never even seen the place."

"I'll bet I know what's going on," Eloise ventured. "You're an actor, aren't you?"

The waiter looked at Eloise for a second and then laughed. "Okay, okay. I confess. I'm guilty. I am an actor, but please don't be mad."

With that, he tugged on the end of his mustache and pulled it off. "I have an audition for the part of a French waiter tomorrow, so I thought I'd get in a little practice tonight. Now, ladies, what can I get you?" He proceeded to take their orders and then left.

"Does that happen a lot around here?" Bess asked.

Eloise smiled and shook her head no. "But many of the waiters in New York are actors, Bess. And a lot of the delivery people, word processors, dog walkers . . . They do many different kinds of work just to survive between acting jobs."

Bess was sobered by the thought that an acting career could be so difficult. But Eloise's words also had a great impact on Nancy.

"Playing different roles," she murmured softly to herself. Suddenly a big piece of the puzzle had fallen into place. That's how the culprit does it, she told herself. Hadn't she herself gone anywhere on the set completely unnoticed in her nurse's uniform? No one had even looked at her twice. Of course! How could she have missed it?

"And when the director called 'action' I was supposed to be sorting these papers at the front desk," Bess was telling Eloise. "And Mattie walks right up to me and says, 'Excuse me. Did Rory Danner leave a message for me?' And I nod and I hand her an envelope. We must have done the scene six times, right, Nancy?" Bess didn't wait for an answer. She just went on, filling Eloise in on every little detail of her big day on "Danner's Dream." Nancy ate her dinner in silence, trying to put the final pieces of the puzzle together.

"I'm stuffed," Bess said as they climbed the stairs to Nancy's aunt's apartment. "That dessert was too much."

"After you girls leave, I'm going to have to go on a diet," Eloise said, reaching into her bag for the keys.

Just then, through the door they heard the phone ring. "Don't worry—the machine will get it," Eloise said, letting them in and flicking the lights on.

"Hello," came Eloise's recorded voice on the answering machine. "I can't come to the phone right now, but if you leave a message at the sound of the beep, I'll get back to you as soon as I can."

"This message is for Nancy Drew." A shiver

ran down Nancy's spine. It was the voice of Lillian Weiss. "It's Lillian, Nancy. There's something I have to tell you. It's a matter of life and death. Meet me on the set tomorrow morning at six o'clock, before rehearsal. I'll leave a pass for you."

Chapter

Fifteen

Nancy, you're not thinking of going, are you?" The color drained from Eloise's face, and she sat down on the sofa. "You told me yourself that you thought this woman might be the killer. I can't allow you to put your life in danger that way, even to save someone else's. You're my niece, and you're the only child my brother has. Think how he would feel if something happened to you!"

Nancy sat down beside her aunt and took her hand. "Aunt Eloise," she said calmly, "ever since I was a little girl, I've been trying to solve mysteries. I can't quit now! It's my life, Aunt Eloise. It's what I do best. Don't ask me to give it up now, please."

Tears in her eyes, Eloise hugged her niece fiercely. "I'll be biting my nails the whole time, you know that?" she said with a resigned laugh. "But why do you have to meet at the studio?"

"Oh, you know how dramatic soap people are. Just a little added mystery. Now, come on, there's nothing to worry about," Nancy countered with a smile. "And besides, I know quite a lot of karate, remember? All those lessons ought to be good for something."

When she got to Worldwide Broadcasting, Nancy picked up her pass at the security desk, then slipped into the main corridor. Every muscle in her body was tensed. There was something wrong about all this—she knew it the moment she had heard Lillian's voice. But something drove her on, step by step, toward the studio.

As she turned down a corridor, she saw someone and ducked back around the corner. It was the janitor, mopping the floors. Not wanting to run into anyone, she went back around, taking the long way to the studio in order to avoid him.

Finally, she reached the vacuum-sealed door and pushed her way in. The set was dimly lit, but Nancy's eyes adjusted to the darkness. At first it seemed to be deserted, but then Nancy saw her.

Lillian was sitting on a chair on the set of the Danner kitchen, holding her head in her hands. As Nancy approached, she turned around.

"Our fair rescuer," she said under her breath. "How kind of you to come." The words were full of bravado, but the old self-assured Lillian was gone. The mocking look had disappeared, and Lillian's face was now fearful.

"Why did you ask me to come here?" Nancy demanded. "What's all this about?"

"Oh, I'm not the maniac, if that's what you're worried about. In fact, I asked you here because—" Lillian's voice wavered. "Because he's after *me* now."

Nancy crossed the room and sat down next to Lillian. Then she listened intently to every word of her story.

"When things started turning weird around here, I got curious. Actually, I was kind of hoping Rick would get what he deserved, if you get my meaning. But then I found something. It was that day I ran into you in the hall. I had just found it in a closet. I didn't want to tell anyone about it, so I hid it where no one would come across it."

"The prop room, of course!" Nancy's eyes

lit up. So that was why Lillian had acted so secretively that day!

"Right. And this little item I found made me want to find out more. So I did. I kept on finding more and more, until—" Lillian's voice was barely a whisper. "Until I got this yesterday." She handed Nancy a typewritten note. "Were you thinking of blackmail, my pet?" it read. "Not if I kill you first."

"So you see," Lillian went on, "that's why I called you here. In case anything happens to me. I mean, I knew you were on the case, and, well, you understand." She picked up a shopping bag that lay at her feet and, taking something out of it, she held it up for Nancy to look at.

"A long-haired wig, glasses, a T-shirt—" Nancy sifted through the contents, her suspicions confirmed. "It looks like a disguise. Whoever it was used it to get around the set unnoticed."

"Exactly," Lillian agreed. "And what better disguise than as a stagehand? One of those anonymous people walking around during every shoot. Everyone else is so busy doing their work, no one notices. It's perfect!"

"What else did you find?" Nancy asked.

"Oh, more of the same. Different every day. I knew immediately that it was an actor. Or an ex-actor—"

Then I was right! Nancy said to herself.

"You see," Lillian went on, "I finally put two and two together. Which, I hate to say, is more than you've done."

"I take it you have proof of the maniac's identity, then," Nancy said.

"Of course I do," she said with a wicked smile. "It is—"

Lillian didn't get a chance to finish her sentence. All of a sudden, every light in the entire studio flashed on. Shading her eyes, Nancy glanced up to the director's booth, where the lighting controls were.

There, looking down at them from behind the thick Plexiglas, was Dwayne Casper! His expression was furious, and in his hand was a gun—pointed straight at Nancy!

Chapter

Sixteen

"WELL, HELLO, YOU two!" Dwayne's voice boomed at them, seeming to come from every imaginable direction. He let out a monstrous laugh. "I only followed Lillian, but I've trapped both of you. How lucky! Congratulations, your death scenes will look so lovely on videotape. A videotape for my personal viewing pleasure only!"

For an instant, Dwayne relaxed his grip on the gun a bit. Nancy, seeing her chance, made a dash for the door. Just as she reached it, she heard it go *whooossshh,* and the red light above it flashed on. The door was locked—vacuum sealed.

"Are we locked up down there?" Dwayne screamed in a grotesque parody of Luther Parks. He laughed again. "A little stage fright, Ms. Elliot? Actually, I didn't know until yesterday that you and Ms. Elliot were one and the same. Very good bit of acting. Very realistic. You see, we strive for realism here—real bullets, real blood, real death." He waved his gun playfully at them.

"You two are only the first act. Rick Arlen's death will be the climax of my little soap opera. He's gotten away from me so far, thanks to you, Nancy Drew. But with you two little nuisances out of the way, I don't think he has much of a chance. Do you?"

Dwayne paused, waiting for a reply. Nancy had to think fast. This might be her only chance to save her life and Lillian's. Somehow she had to distract him, make him forget he had a gun.

"Dwayne, why? Why do you hate Rick so much? Lillian and Mattie have more reason to hate him than you do!"

Her words seemed to ignite Dwayne's fury. He exploded at her, just as he had at Bess that day in his office.

"More reason than I? What do you know about it? Keep your ignorant little mouth shut! Rick Arlen has to die, and I'll tell you why. Because he killed me, that's why. He killed Dwayne Casper."

Dwayne paused for breath. Nancy had the feeling Dwayne's story was a long one. That was good. She needed time—time to think of a way out.

"I was an actor," Dwayne cried, all the hurt and rage in him pouring out with his story. "I'd studied every aspect of my craft and was a master of Shakespeare, dialects, stage combat—everything. I was underrated and underappreciated—but brilliant. Then I met Mattie.

"We fell in love, and I was the happiest man on earth. Then—then came August. We did *Romeo and Juliet*. Mattie was Juliet, but Rick beat me out for the role of Romeo. The director was a sucker for a pretty face, and so, I soon found out, was Mattie.

"From that moment on, my life was never the same. And I never forgot what he had done to me."

As Dwayne ranted on, Nancy looked around desperately for some way out.

"I am not like some people, who fall in love every day," he rasped. "When I lost Mattie, I knew that I would never love anyone ever again. I decided that if I couldn't have her, I'd make money, lots of money. I gave up acting and became an agent instead.

"I made them stars. I did it all. And how did Rick pay me back? By leaving me, that's how. I got nothing in return for all my hard work—nothing at all. He had destroyed me again.

"Once Rick left, other clients began to leave. All I had left was Mattie. And then—" Dwayne paused, and his expression grew dark with rage. "Then he started luring Mattie away from me. That's when I decided to kill him. Which brings me back—" he raised the gun at Nancy, looking down at them "—to you two ladies."

"Dwayne!" Nancy shouted, shaking him out of his daze. "Your story sounds like a soap opera. That stuff doesn't happen in real life!"

"That shows what you know about life, Nancy Drew," Dwayne rasped into the mike. "Real life *is* a soap opera. You'll learn that. Or rather, you would have, had you lived."

"Rick didn't kill you," Nancy insisted. "You're still—"

Dwayne erupted again. "Enough!" he screamed. "It's time for the final closeup. I'm going to write you two out of the script forever."

Quickly, he disappeared from sight. Nancy guessed that he was on his way down to the set. That only gave her a few seconds to think of something.

Nancy looked frantically around. Lillian was standing, shocked, unable to help in any way. She was frozen with fear. As clever as she had been in figuring out who the criminal was, she was utterly useless right then.

In the few seconds she had left, Nancy scanned the set, looking for something —anything. Then, she saw it.

Over in the corner stood a large metal cylinder. On it were written the words "Smoke Machine." Rushing over to it, Nancy found the control switch and turned it to the Dense setting.

Not a moment too soon, either. Seemingly from nowhere, Dwayne appeared.

"Ah, there you are, my nosy little friend. Would you care to rejoin Ms. Weiss onstage?"

Nancy moved slowly back to the kitchen area, hoping that her plan would work.

"What's that hissing?" Dwayne turned and looked around nervously, but all he could see was the nearer half of the studio. The rest was hidden by a thick white fog, which was made even worse by the spotlights.

Quickly, while his back was turned, Nancy grabbed Lillian by the arm and pulled her into the protection of the fog. By the time Dwayne realized what was happening and turned around again, they were gone!

Dwayne cursed loudly as Nancy dragged Lillian into a foggy corner on the set. She left Lillian there and began to walk toward the sound of Dwayne's voice. She had to get the jump on him from behind.

Then she heard a sound that made her heart sink. It was the sound of a giant fan—the wind machine.

"Very clever, Nancy Drew," came Dwayne's voice through the diminishing fog. "But there's an antidote for every poison, or vice versa."

The fog was now down to a very small area, and Nancy knew that her time was running out. Crouching down, she took a deep breath and prepared to make a desperate dive at Dwayne. He would still have the gun, she knew. She had only one advantage—surprise.

Rearing back, Nancy flung herself through the air at Dwayne. At the last moment, he turned and saw her. The two of them fell together, toppling over each other, and Dwayne's gun emptied itself.

Chapter

Seventeen

THOSE WERE GUNSHOTS coming from the set!"

"Quick, this way!"

When the police raced onto the set they found Dwayne Casper flat on the floor. On top of him was Nancy Drew, holding his arms in a double hammerlock.

"His gun is on the floor over there," she told the police breathlessly as they relieved her of her burden.

"Nancy!" Eloise exclaimed, rushing over to her.

"I'm fine, really, Aunt Eloise."

"Well, all the karate lessons in the world

143

wouldn't have helped if this bullet had come any closer!" Eloise poked at the sleeve of Nancy's jacket. In it was a charred round hole the size of a dime.

Nancy looked down at the hole, her heart skipping a beat. "Please, don't tell Dad," she begged. "And I promise I'll be more careful from now on."

Throwing her arms around her niece, Eloise sighed. "Oh, Nancy, I'm just glad you're alive!"

Bess rushed up to them and threw her arms over theirs in a three-way hug. "Thank goodness, you're all right!" she cried. "When we heard the shots—" She couldn't go on.

The police had handcuffed Dwayne, who stood there passively, a dull look in his eye.

"Do you know how close I was to paying Arlen back for all he's done to me?" he began telling the police officer, who stood impassively beside him clutching his arm. "Do you know how long I worked to get this close?" Dwayne muttered bitterly, his hands locked behind his back.

"Tell your story to the sergeant, buddy," the police officer said. "Ms. Drew, I'll need to get a statement from you and from Ms. Weiss. Would you see that she makes it down to the station house?"

"Of course," Nancy agreed. In all the commotion, she hadn't even given a thought to Lillian. Apparently, the fright had been a bit too much for her—she'd fainted.

"I *had* to call the police, Nancy," Eloise was explaining. "Something told me you weren't safe, and I had to."

At the door, Dwayne spun around suddenly. "Rick Arlen was going to die. He should have died! And I would have killed him if it hadn't been for you, Nancy Drew!"

"Whew." Bess sighed as the officer pushed Dwayne outside. "He's crazy—"

"He's in the right hands now," Nancy added soberly. "And not a moment too soon, either."

"Flight four-seventeen will be boarding at gate three in five minutes."

"That's our flight, Aunt Eloise," said Nancy, putting down her luggage so she could give her aunt a hug.

"You must promise me you'll come again soon—maybe in the fall?" Eloise asked. "And give your father my love, will you? Goodbye, Bess—I hope I'll see you again soon."

But when Nancy and Bess turned to go, they heard their names being called out.

"Nancy! Bess, wait!" A familiar voice floated down the airport corridor. Turning around, Nancy saw a radiant Mattie Jensen running toward them, her auburn curls flying around her face. "We couldn't let you leave without saying goodbye," she cried.

Beside her, Rick Arlen was cradling two large bouquets of roses in his arms. He handed the first to Nancy and said, "Thank you for saving my life, Nancy—I don't know what I would have done without you."

Then he turned to Bess, who seemed more than a little flustered. "This one is for you, love," he murmured, giving her the flowers.

"Oh, Rick, thank you," she cried, letting down her guard. For a minute, Nancy almost felt sorry that she had been thinking of him as such a heel. She was sure the flowers were his way of saying he was sorry for toying with Bess's emotions.

But the hopeful light went out of her eyes when he explained, "They're from Pappas. He asked us to give them to you."

"Pappas sent us flowers?" asked Nancy incredulously.

"Oh, he's really a teddy bear," said Mattie. "And he's on top of the world now that the show's back on track."

"He even agreed to cancel my contract with no hard feelings," Rick said, laughing. "In fact, he's already written it into the script. I'm getting killed next week, and I go to work on my feature the week after. Ironic, isn't it? Rick Arlen lives, but Rory Danner bites the dust!"

"And Pappas rehired everyone that he

fired," Mattie added. "All thanks to you, Nancy."

Nancy's eyes twinkled. Nothing beat the wonderful feeling she always had after solving a case. "I'm glad I could be of some help," was all she could say.

"But the best news of all is—" Rick flashed Mattie a million-dollar smile. "Shall I tell them, or do you want to?"

Mattie beamed. "You go ahead."

"Mattie has agreed to marry me," he announced proudly. "We're flying to her parents' house next weekend. All this made me realize that there's only one woman in the world for me." He looked somber for a moment, adding, "Thank goodness it wasn't too late."

Nancy noticed that Rick avoided Bess's eyes as he spoke. "Well," Nancy said, "that's great news, you two. Congratulations." Looking over at her friend, Nancy could tell that Bess wished she were in Mattie's shoes. "Well, we'd better get going, though," Nancy said. "See you next time we're in New York!"

With that, and a final squeeze of her aunt's hand, Nancy put her arm around Bess's shoulders and walked past the Passengers Only sign.

"I'm sorry it worked out like this, Bess," she told her friend. News like that had to hurt.

"Oh, it's okay," Bess said and sighed. "I'm just so tired."

Nancy adjusted the strap of her carry-on bag

with a weary smile. "I know what you mean. After a vacation like this, we really need a vacation!"

"So tell me," said George, leaning forward over a hot fudge sundae and crinkling her nose. "Is Rick Arlen really as gorgeous in real life as he is on TV?"

Nancy looked over at Bess, wondering how she would respond.

"Not nearly," Bess replied. "He's kind of short, and those fabulous blue eyes are really contacts."

Nancy rolled her eyes. Bess was laying it on just a little thick.

"And you actually had a date with him?" George was practically shouting. Bess just turned her face away. "I can't believe it!" George went on. "I'm so jealous! What was he like? What did you do?"

"Uh, George—she doesn't want to talk about it," Nancy warned, finally able to interrupt.

"Oh, I get it." George nodded. "Well, you did get to be on television—and on 'Danner's Dream,'" she exclaimed cheerfully.

"Yeah—" Bess sighed. "But seeing how actors and actresses really live, and how hard they work, I don't know. I've been thinking of becoming a model instead." With that, she took an enormous mouthful of strawberry ice cream.

"Oh, really?" Nancy said skeptically. "Will you go on your famous ice cream diet?"

"She's got to look her sundae best," quipped George in reply.

Bess, however, was not amused. "Lay off, you two, will you?" she said testily. "I'm depressed enough as it is."

"Sorry, Bess," said Nancy. "There'll be other guys."

"Not for me," Bess insisted, shaking her head vehemently. "I'm through with men forever." She put down her spoon and gazed out the window dejectedly.

Suddenly her attention was caught by someone passing in front of the window—someone tall, male, and very good-looking. "Hey, who is *that?*" she asked eagerly. "He must be new in town. I never would have missed someone like that."

But neither George nor Nancy could answer. Both of them were doubled up with laughter.

Same old Bess!

Nancy's next case:

The River Heights Country Club is a playground for the town's wealthier citizens. But lately those citizens have been getting ripped off!

When Nancy investigates the robbery of a be-jeweled necklace, she finds out why: The country club members love to talk about their valuable possessions; the club is the perfect place for thieves to learn what—and where—to steal.

It seems the thieves have also been hearing about Nancy Drew. Almost before she starts the case, she finds herself in danger. Can Nancy get the goods on this ring of thieves? Find out in *CIRCLE OF EVIL*, Case #18 in The Nancy Drew Files™.

BOOK ONE: BRING DOWN THE NIGHT

It started with a fur coat. Lana thought it was a gift, but there were strings attached, and they led straight to a man who wouldn't take no for an answer. The situation is beyond her charm, and she's scared. Enter the Pink Flamingos. Together they confront the man, uncovering the dark side that lurks beneath the elegant surface of Palm Beach—and blow the lid off a million-dollar scam.

Pink Flamingos

GET IT...
AT YOUR LOCAL BOOKSTORE

A Simon & Schuster Graphic Novel
Pink Flamingos is a trademark of Angel Entertainment, Inc.

- -

HAVE YOU SEEN NANCY DREW® LATELY?

Nancy Drew has become a girl of the 80's!
There is hardly a girl from seven to seventeen
who doesn't know her name.

THE NANCY DREW FILES™

- # 1 SECRETS CAN KILL 64193/$2.75
- # 2 DEADLY INTENT 64393/$2.75
- # 3 MURDER ON ICE 64194/$2.75
- # 4 SMILE AND SAY MURDER 64585/$2.75
- # 5 HIT AND RUN HOLIDAY 64394/$2.75
- # 6 WHITE WATER TERROR 64586/$2.75
- # 7 DEADLY DOUBLES 62543/$2.75
- # 8 TWO POINTS FOR MURDER 63079/$2.75
- # 9 FALSE MOVES 63076/$2.75
- #10 BURIED SECRETS 63077/$2.75
- #11 HEART OF DANGER 63078/$2.75
- #12 FATAL RANSOM 62644/$2.75
- #13 WINGS OF FEAR 64137/ $2.75
- #14 THIS SIDE OF EVIL 64139/$2.75
- #15 TRIAL BY FIRE 64139/$2.75
- #16 NEVER SAY DIE 64140/$2.75
- #17 STAY TUNED
      FOR DANGER 64141/$2.75